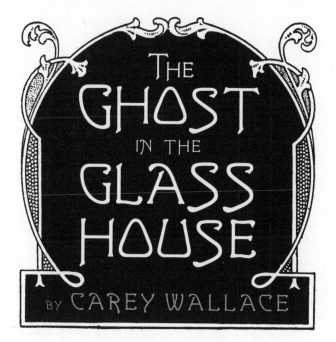

THE GHOST IN THE GLASS HOUSE

BY CAREY WALLACE

CLARION BOOKS

HOUGHTON MIFFLIN HARCOURT
BOSTON   NEW YORK

CLARION BOOKS

215 Park Avenue South, New York, New York 10003

Clarion Books is an imprint of
Houghton Mifflin Harcourt Publishing Company.

www.hmhbooks.com

The text was set in Goudy Old Style.
Book design by Sharismar Rodriguez

Library of Congress Cataloging-in-Publication Data
Wallace, Carey, 1974–
The ghost in the glass house / Carey Wallace.
pages cm
Summary: In a seaside New England town in the 1920s, twelve-year-old Clare finds refuge
from the cruelty of her society friends in a mysterious glass house inhabited by Jack, a
charming and playful ghost who cannot remember his real name or how he died.
ISBN 978-0-544-02291-1 (hardback)
[1. Ghosts—Fiction. 2. Aristocracy (Social class)—Fiction.
3. Mothers and daughters—Fiction. 4. New England—History—20th century—Fiction.]
I. Title.
PZ7.W15474Gho 2013
[Fic]—dc23   2012051330

Manufactured in the United States of America
DOC 10 9 8 7 6 5 4 3 2 1
4500427447

for Alexandra and Daniel

The going from a world we know
To one a wonder still
Is like the child's adversity
Whose vista is a hill,
Behind the hill is sorcery,
And everything unknown,
But will the secret compensate
For climbing it alone?

—Emily Dickinson

ONE

CLARE FITZGERALD HAD SEEN SO MUCH in
the twelve short years of her life that she could
almost always guess what was going to happen next.

So when she came around the side of their new summer
home and saw the strange glass house winking at her from
the stand of trees at the foot of the yard, she was caught
between two feelings. She knew the first one well: the annoyance of a seasoned traveler who is confronted by a cabaret
that has just opened at an address where she expected to find
a reputable bank, or a reputable bank that has just opened
at the address of a former cabaret. The other feeling, just
as strong, took her longer to name because it was so rare.
But after a moment she admitted to herself that it might be
wonder: a deep thrill of suspicion that, despite everything
she and her mother had seen, they had not yet exhausted all
the world's mysteries and treasures.

At first glance, the glass house was a riot of reflections: sky and cloud, white brick, the pale underbellies of leaves. Then it resolved into a simple dome held together by copper beams gone green from exposure to wind and rain. It sat about fifty paces from the big white brick house she and her mother were moving into that day. A stand of young maples shaded the glass walls, which were further screened by climbing roses that crept all the way up to the slanted panes of the roof.

As a rule, Clare preferred to take her pleasures in small doses, bit by bit, instead of gulping them down whole, as her mother did. Under normal circumstances, she might have circled the whole yard, inspected the surrounding gardens, and taken the measure of the glass house from a dozen different vantage points before she made her approach. But sometimes life forced her to make exceptions. Today was one of them.

Clare had escaped only a few minutes earlier, in the confusion surrounding the arrival at their new summer home. If she lingered too long now in any one place, her mother would almost certainly take her captive again. Clare didn't know when she'd be able to get away next. And she'd never seen anything like the strange glass house glinting in the trees.

She glanced down briefly at the uncomfortable velvet and cardboard slippers her mother had insisted she wear on the train, with the cheerful hope that they might suffer some mortal damage in the course of her explorations. Then she cut straight down the substantial rise where the big white house was set and crossed the rolling lawn, through silver magnolias, redbud, and disheveled lilacs, to the grove that sheltered the glass house.

Under the maple branches, the air was filled with bits of pollen that glowed like tiny embers. As her eyes adjusted to the shade, she realized that the glass house didn't have corners like other buildings: it was an octagon, eight sides fastened together, so that the room it formed was more like a circle than a square. The leaves of the climbing roses were so thick that she couldn't see anything inside: just tantalizing flashes of color blurred by the glass.

Furthermore, it didn't seem to have a door.

Clare started around one side, found nothing but wide panes covered with vines, then doubled back. Her brow had begun to furrow with disbelief and frustration when, on the far side from the big house on the hill, she discovered a narrow pane of glass, about the height of a man, not so overgrown with vines as the rest. Unlike all the other glass, which was weather-stained but unmarked, this pane was etched with an oval pattern so intricate that Clare thought she saw half a dozen false letters in the crabbed loops and curls. But when she looked closer, none of them resolved into actual words.

A moment later, she discovered the handle of the door, half hidden by the same vines that curled over the mossy flagstone at her feet and met in a canopy over the green copper door frame.

The handle was copper green as well, more like a paddle than a knob. She turned it down to release the latch as she peered through her own reflection at the mysterious shapes inside.

The door didn't budge.

She pulled the handle up. No luck.

Then she saw a small neat cut in the embellished metal below the handle: a keyhole.

The glass house was locked.

Frowning in concentration, Clare circled the building, looking for a key box or a hiding rock or even a stray garden fork with tines long enough to tease the lock open. When she didn't find any of these, she settled on a short hardwood twig, about the same size as a bone from her hand. She hunched under the handle and fiddled the twig this way and that, listening for the telltale click of the mechanism as it swung free, a trick she had learned a few summers before when her mother had befriended the ship's detective on a trip across the Atlantic.

The ship's detective was a pale, gangly scholar with a boy's face and prematurely gray hair who had been given the job by his uncle, a member of the shipping company's board, due to his complete unsuitability for any other work. He'd spent the voyage under the misconception that Clare found his responsibilities as a detective boring while her mother found them fascinating: an almost perfect inversion of the truth. As a result, he would only speak to Clare's mother about his work when he believed Clare was asleep. So Clare had spent the week feigning sleeping fits on the lounge chairs of the second deck as he regaled her mother with the exploits and methods of the modern bank robber, jewel thief, and bootlegger, all of which he'd culled from various publications on the topic and not from personal experience, which he spent the bulk of his formidable intelligence trying to avoid. But despite Clare's rapt attention on those bright afternoons, the lock on the door to the glass house held fast.

Clare dropped the twig into the glossy myrtle that hid the roots of the roses, cupped her hands around her eyes, and pressed her face to the glass.

Inside, the vines cast gnarled shadows over a confusion of furniture arranged on overlapping oriental rugs, which produced a visual effect so jumbled that for a moment Clare couldn't tell where anything began and anything else ended. The sun, with no interference from shutters or drapes, had taken its toll on all the fabrics, brightening some, erasing others. Now, at full noon, it made the whites blaze. Piercing glints shot from the domed case of an anniversary clock and the tarnished surface of a silver vase. Then a hodgepodge of mismatched, castaway pieces began to fall into place: a pair of mulberry leather smoking chairs. A delicate sea-green divan with a back that swelled up over the curve of the seat like a wave about to crash on the beach. A low table with several mysterious drawers. A buffet crowned by the anniversary clock and vase, cluttered with candlesticks and books. And, just to the left of the locked door, the black shadow of a grand piano, positioned so that the player would play with her back to the big house, looking through the propped cover into the half-tamed forest that overtook the yard a few strides beyond.

Clare glanced up at the big house to make sure she had not been discovered, then pressed her face back to the door, half surprised to find that everything inside remained just as it had been. The glass house was so strange that she wouldn't have blinked at seeing exotic birds now perched on the piano lid, or all the furniture suddenly replaced by a scrap of a white desert, with a lone Bedouin disappearing in the distance.

She'd learned about the desert from one of her mother's friends, Mr. Pedersen, after his visit to Arabia, and she had been captivated by his claim that in the desert, the silence was so complete that he had spent an entire leg of one solitary journey singing aloud to reassure himself that he had not gone deaf. Since then, she had begun to imagine a desert that could appear to her anywhere, like a reverse mirage, whenever their travels overwhelmed her. As she and her mother rushed to catch a train that shuddered and hissed in preparation for departure, Clare would look up at the mirrored windows of a sleeping car and suddenly know that a beautiful desert lay within, in full darkness, complete with stars, but without a sound except the sand that whispered underfoot. Or as she followed her mother down the dim hall of a club for lunch, shivering under the thin taffeta of a fancy dress, she'd catch sight of a few grains of white sand spilling through the crack of a closed door: a sure sign that the strong desert sun waited for her within. Once or twice she'd actually struggled down the length of a train or snuck into a club's private rooms to test these intimations and found only a Pullman bunk and an empty library. But these disappointments didn't discourage her. Instead, they felt like clues: false leads crossed off a list that would one day bring her to the edge of the real desert, wherever it lay in wait.

Still, the glass house remained resolutely as it had been. Clare straightened and let the sun blot out the room with the reflection of trees and sky. She tapped idly at the glass, three impatient raps with the tip of her index finger.

A moment later, as if in answer to Clare's absent scrap of code, the glass tapped back.

Instantly, Clare cupped her hands and pressed her face to the door.

Inside, everything stood exactly as it had. The only motion she could catch was a shiver in the shadows as wind stirred the leaves overhead. She looked for anything that might have knocked against the glass: a loose chain, a trapped bird. If something had, she couldn't see it.

"Hm," she said aloud.

She narrowed her eyes, her face still pressed to the glass. Then she tapped again, more deliberately: one, two, three.

This time, when the glass tapped back, the vibrations tingled in her forehead and palms.

She sprang away. For a few breaths, she glared at her own reflection, tangled in the weird etching.

Then she lifted her chin to hide her fear and ran back up the hill to the big house.

Two

HAT MORNING, AT THE train station, Clare's mother had hired four cabs and filled their unoccupied seats and the gaping maws of their trunks with the various pieces of her three sets of luggage: the rich brown cordovan; the alligators Mr. Pedersen had shot himself, gotten made into a set of valises and hatboxes, and shipped to her from Florida as a gift; and the light blue Italian silk that bore faint traces of every raindrop that had ever fallen on it. All four cabs had pulled into the drive that wound along the side of their new summer place just as their new houseman emerged from the kitchen door, squinting against the afternoon sun.

"That must be Mack," Clare's mother had told her. "He's the one who sent all the wires."

Clare had watched him as the car rolled to a stop and her mother fished a knot of bills out of her clutch. His graying hair was cropped close, but not close enough to disguise a stubborn curl. His stance was solid. A gold ring glinted on his left hand.

Their cabbie opened the rear door for Clare's mother. Clare scrambled out after her.

With eerie precision, the other three cabbies emerged from their vehicles and leaned back against them to indicate that, in their opinion, their job was now done. With a curt nod at Clare's mother, Mack folded his arms and stepped aside from the kitchen door to indicate that, in his opinion, their job had only just begun. The first cabbie, who had only ferried his passengers and their personal bags, smelled trouble. His fare and tip already in hand, he darted back to his car, spun it around the circle drive, and headed for the open road.

Clare's mother had broken the impasse by beginning to thank everyone involved before they had actually done anything. Her pretty square heels wobbling on the drive's shifting sand, she'd pulled open the back door of the next cab and gamely begun to yank at a cordovan trunk that was big enough to hold two of her.

"Thank you so much," she told the cab's owner breathlessly. "I don't know what we would have done without you. Nobody ought to have this much luggage. Every time they push it up a gangplank I ask them to please throw half of it into the sea, but no one ever listens to me. Clare?" she said. She stepped back and nodded at the shining blood-red trunk, which, despite the considerable dramatic effect of her efforts, hadn't budged. Familiar with the game, Clare rushed up, caught the silver handle with both hands, and leaned back with all her might. To both her and her mother's surprise, the trunk slid about a foot along the rough upholstery of the back seat, knocking Clare off balance. She crashed into her mother. The two of them gazed at each other in shock.

But their charade had already proven too much for the cabbie. "Well, no, ma'am," he said, ducking his head to Clare's mother and swatting Clare out of the way. "Let me get these for you."

When his will broke, the general strike collapsed. Down the line, the other cabbies popped their doors and filled their arms with suitcases and twine-wrapped boxes. Mack gave up his high ground on the kitchen step, swung a baby-blue trunk onto his own shoulder, and led them inside. When they all emerged from the house again, their faces red and glossy with sweat, a woman had joined the little parade. Almost a whole head taller than Mack, she wore a blue and white striped dress with a crisp white apron, her gray hair pulled back matter-of-factly from her smooth face, her frame thin but sturdy, like an old trellis that has outlasted the brief lives of countless roses.

At the sight of her, Clare's mother broke into the delighted, inviting smile that had won them entry to so many parties, swept them up so many gangplanks, and opened the doors of so many fine homes. "You must be Tilda," she said. "I'm Cynthia."

Tilda looked at Clare's mother as if she were a spill on the floor that she would worry about after she put out a fire on the stove, seized a giant trunk, and vanished into the kitchen.

As Clare's mother struggled to recover from this rough treatment, Clare had seen her opening. She dove into the cavernous back seat of the nearest cab, retrieved a hatbox and a jewelry case from the package tray, and scampered after the servants.

Inside, the kitchen was deserted, and flooded with noon light. Someone had propped open the door to the dining room with a metal bucket of dirty potatoes. Clare darted through. Since she no longer needed the jewelry case and hatbox as props to make her escape, she abandoned them temporarily under the dining room table. Then she glanced around. Down a long hall, she caught a glimpse of blue sky through a tall oval window in the front door.

She stopped for a moment on the threshold of the hall to listen. Voices drifted down the staircase that led up to the second floor, still faint enough that the fragments she heard only added up to nonsense.

"Look at this cinnamon island!" one of them ordered.

"But I don't like dancing in the snow," the other complained.

In a flash, Clare had flown down the hall, out the new door, and across the lawn. She'd caught sight of the glass house as soon as she rounded the corner.

But now, when she ran back up the hill and circled the house to the drive, all three cabs were gone. The only hint that they had ever been there at all was a few faint clouds of yellow dust that still hung over the drive's gray pebbles. The kitchen door was shut.

Clare went in without knocking.

She had hoped that all the adults would still be upstairs, locked in combat with the contents of her mother's trunks, which could take even the most seasoned maid a week to sort out. But when Clare stepped into the kitchen again, Tilda stood at a high worktable in the center of the room, trimming a handful of yellow roses.

Clare's sudden appearance didn't slow her busy fingers even for a moment.

"I see you've had a tour of the yard," Tilda said.

Clare nodded, watching for a sign of what tack to take with this new maid. A friendly porter could make the most cramped quarters feel like home, and an unhappy maid could make a lavish apartment unlivable. So Clare's first project on arriving in any new place was to size up the servants and adopt whatever pose would disarm them. Some people liked to meet a girl with an air of wondering innocence. Others, she had learned, preferred a clever young lady. And there were a number of useful shades in between.

Tilda made a quick cut at the base of each rose and dropped the yellow blossoms into a jet vase, where they quivered from the shock as she turned her attention to a bundle of white phlox. Her plain face gave nothing away.

Beginning with a compliment was almost always safe. "The grounds are beautiful," Clare ventured. "I don't know when we've been in a place this pretty." This wasn't true. Charm was her mother's primary condition for picking the establishments where they stayed, whether or not the pipes worked, or the fireplaces choked, or the roof still had enough spirit to keep the rain out. Clare had lived in a suite of rooms where blue sky had been hand-painted on every ceiling by a visiting Italian; in an apartment overlooking the Seine where their extraordinary view had almost made up for the stench of the river; and in a hut with sheer mosquito-net walls built on stilts a dozen feet above the warm waters of the Mediterranean. That particular complex of scarves and twigs had been connected to land only by rickety rope-and-board breezeways lit at night by torches whose flames, reflected on the dark water, made the whole surf seem molten.

One morning they'd woken to discover that a stray spark had reduced the fragile bridge that connected them with the mainland to a few scraps of charred wreckage floating in the turquoise shallows below. Her mother had laughed, used the scrap of wood that remained as a diving board, and swum to land, where she'd ordered her breakfast served on the restaurant's patio so her wet hair could dry in the sun. But Clare, afraid to dive from that height despite her mother's entreaties, had waited alone in the windy hut all morning until the men from the hotel constructed a makeshift ramp sturdy enough to lure her back to land. Every place Clare had ever lived had been at least as pretty as this. Still, the compliment was a reliable one.

Tilda raised her eyebrows, selected one long stem of phlox from among the rest, circled her finger around it just under the blooms, and with a single deft stroke denuded it of all its tender leaves.

Once Clare established what kind of person she was dealing with, most people were no harder to unlock than a traveling trunk. The key had to be carefully chosen, though. A compliment that might charm a person who wanted to be liked could insult a person who wanted respect. Showing too much respect to a person who wanted to be liked might make them wonder whether you liked them at all.

And Tilda, so far, had given no hint as to which category she belonged in.

Unable to settle on a strategy, Clare gave in to curiosity. "I saw the glass house," she said. "But it's locked."

Tilda cleaned another stem of phlox. "Yes," she said. "Last year's girl was in the habit of meeting her young man there. She hid the key so they wouldn't be surprised, and since she left, no one can find it."

This was quite a bit more than Clare was used to being told. Servants, as a rule, were excellent sources of information, but you could almost never find out anything by asking outright. The trick was to hang around the pantry or the sewing room long enough that they forgot she was there and began to speak freely. This principle held true, actually, for all adults, although Clare was perpetually surprised by how quickly they lost track of the fact that she was a thinking person just like them and not another piece of furniture or an interesting plant.

She watched Tilda closely, unsure if the moment of frankness was some freak phenomenon or the first plume of smoke that signaled a spectacular geyser buried deep within.

Tilda laid the stems of cleaned phlox side by side, brought the ends even, trimmed them, and distributed the white blooms among the yellow roses.

In her mind, Clare turned the locked glass house over like a puzzle box, while all the furniture inside tumbled this way and that.

The only flowers that remained on the high table were a half dozen pale blue Dutch iris. Tilda sliced their stems, lifted them as a bunch, and gave them a good shake. Then, as if she were doing nothing more than throwing down the second-best silverware for a weekday dinner, she dropped the blue blossoms among the roses and phlox and scattered the sword blades of the iris leaves between them.

The effect, despite Clare's long acquaintance with beauty, was breathtaking.

The light that flared in Tilda's eyes only betrayed her for an instant. Then she steadied her expression with the air of a practiced liar, picked up the vase, and carried the jostling stems out of the kitchen.

THREE

CLARE TRAILED AFTER HER only seconds later, but when she reached the dining room, Tilda had already set the bouquet on the buffet and disappeared. Clare checked under the broad oval table. The hatbox and jewelry case were still safely hidden between the varnished wooden legs. She retrieved them, stepped into the hall, and listened again. Voices still drifted from the rooms above.

This time, she followed them up the stairs. Sunshine poured onto the wide landing through three tall windows that overlooked the front yard. Two doors led off the landing. One, immediately to Clare's right at the top of the stairs, was shut. The other, on the opposite side of the landing, stood open.

"Clare, thank God," her mother said when Clare crossed the landing and appeared in the open door. "I'm driving poor Mr. Burlingham crazy. You've got to help him."

"Just Mack," Mack said, with a note of pleading in his

voice that suggested this wasn't the first time he'd made the request.

Clare's mother stood in the middle of a sunny room, surrounded by towers of mismatched luggage and an assortment of items which, for mysterious reasons, had already found their way out of the various trunks. A small porcelain elephant marched solemnly across a cloud of red tissue on the nightstand. Mack held a hat trimmed with peacock feathers gingerly in both hands, as if it had already made one attempt at flight and he wasn't sure it could be trusted again. A heap of party dresses in Easter-egg colors seemed to be recovering from a dead faint on the bed.

Like so many rooms in seaside resorts, this one was done in white and blue: a white seahorse woven in relief on the white crewel bedspread, pert blue sailboats frozen at merry angles on the upholstered chair by the window. But stubborn traces of earlier residents remained. A small bookshelf in the corner was crammed with what could only be a personal collection: dozens of volumes shoved together, some missing covers, some upside down, in no discernible order. On the far side of the room, a pair of wooden wardrobes stood open, one already half full of dresses too dark and unfashionable to be her mother's.

"We brought everything in here," Clare's mother told

her. "And I thought, of course Clare will be next door." She paused for effect. "But there *is* no next door."

Clare was accustomed to taking her mother's impossible dilemmas in stride, but this was actually news. The two of them always slept in communicating rooms: it was one of the excuses her mother used to keep her more importunate suitors at bay, and it allowed Clare to pad into her mother's room anytime she wanted. Even though Clare rarely did, the nearness of her mother's room was one of the only shreds of home she still had.

Surprised, Clare frowned.

"You see?" Clare's mother exclaimed to Mack. He looked at her in confusion, then made an attempt at a sympathetic nod, an expression somewhat marred by the unmistakable traces of his true feeling, which came closer to the uneasiness of a scientist becoming acquainted with the surprising volatility of a new compound.

Clare's mother turned back to Clare. "There are two rooms across the hall," she said. "One of them's lovely. It looks over the back garden. But the other one . . ." She trailed off, apparently unable to find the words.

"It was a boy's room," Mack offered by way of apology.

"Look," Clare's mother said. She swept gracefully through the maze of luggage, caught Clare's hand, and pulled her across the landing to the closed door at the head of the stairs.

Clare's mother threw the door open to reveal a spacious room with a blue and green tartan on the bed, a dresser, and a desk. A small oval mirror hung over the dresser, cinder gray with age. Its twin hung on the opposite wall, so the two mirrors reflected each other in endless dwindling replicas. A somewhat clumsily built model of a ship at full sail was becalmed below one mirror on the dresser's glassy mahogany. A few hand-colored illustrations had been pinned to the wall nearby: an ocean battle with several proud ships in flames, and a tiger, reared back on his hind legs like a charging stallion, who bore so little resemblance to the actual tigers Clare had seen that she wondered if the artist had ever seen one himself, or worked only from stories or dreams.

Clare's mother shivered expressively. "So you see," she said. She closed that door, then crossed back to her own room, but didn't stop there. Instead, she followed a narrow band of the landing that ran from her room toward the rear of the house, and a third door. This one opened on a cozy room built into the slope of the roof.

"What do you think?" Clare's mother said. This was a real question, not for effect. Her voice was low and serious, as it was when Clare was sick.

Clare stepped inside. The wall behind the bed was papered with a life-size illustration of a birch forest in gold afternoon light. A pale yellow and green quilt covered the bed. A wicker swing stuffed with cushions hung at the window in the gable nook. Down in the yard, the irregular stands of iris were reduced to daubs of black and orange and blue. The panes of the glass house glinted through the maple leaves.

"I like it," Clare said.

Clare's mother slipped a hand around Clare's waist and rested her cheek on the top of Clare's head.

"Are you sure?" she asked.

Clare nodded.

"I just got so tired of camping in places where no one really *lives*," her mother said, her voice still low. "All the other summer houses here are out on the water, but this one was a real home once. You can tell, because the decorating is terrible. But that might be a relief, don't you think?"

Clare's skin prickled. Since the last time their cab had pulled away from the house she grew up in, almost three years ago, Clare had wanted to go home. But even then, she had known better than to ask. Pestering her mother to do anything only strengthened her resolve against it, so a campaign to go home would only delay their return. All Clare could do was wait for the mysterious winds in her mother's mind to shift. And in the last three years, this was the closest her mother had ever come to admitting that she might share Clare's homesickness.

Clare barely dared to move, seized by a gambler's hope. She knew the odds against her, but the chance to win swept all other thoughts away.

"We could go home," Clare ventured. "If you're tired of hotels."

Instantly, her mother's hand rose from Clare's shoulder.

"Oh, darling," she said. "New York in the summer? Haven't the social reformers been trying to pass some kind of law against that?"

Clare searched her mother's face, but her features had already settled into a bright mask. Her mouth twisted faintly at her own joke. Her blond hair, waved around her face, glowed almost white, as it always did in sunlight. Her pale blue eyes were perfectly distant.

She kissed Clare's forehead and went out into the hall.

"Mack," she called. "Clare has saved our lives."

Still at the window, Clare stared down at the garden, warped and bent by the old glass.

She raised her hand and tapped three times, but no one answered.

FOUR

CLARE'S FRIEND BRIDGET ANSWERED the door of the shingled mansion her parents had taken for the summer herself. She was wearing a sleeveless lavender party dress covered with vines picked out in silver sequins, despite the fact that it was eleven o'clock in the morning. The gown hung loose on her, a dead giveaway that she'd rescued another castoff of her mother's, although Clare knew better than to point this out.

"Clare," Bridget said. "I was afraid you'd been taken by bandits on your way through the wilderness. How did your mother ever find a place that's not even on the shore?"

She stepped aside to let Clare pass into a wide entry hall dominated by a round wooden table inlaid with mother-of-pearl in the shape of a compass rose. On the far side of the room, two sets of French doors opened on a screened porch. Beyond the screen the ocean gleamed.

"Do you have any Visitors?" Clare asked, to take revenge for Bridget's slight to Clare's mother. *Visitors* was what

Bridget's mother called the spirits, intimations, and presences that had shared the homes Bridget's family had occupied over the years. Clare's intense interest in these Visitors was a source of gratification to Bridget's mother and a point of contention with Bridget, who thought about ghosts very much the same way that most people thought about God: despite the fact that they were probably real, it was unforgivably impolite to talk about them.

Bridget turned on her heel and headed for the porch. "The house is free," she said over her shoulder, meaning that her mother's current Sensitive hadn't detected any spirits yet this season.

The porch was furnished with white wicker stuffed with yellow cushions and pillows. A bouquet of sea-garden flowers, also white and yellow, stood on a low table, the foot of its vase filled with wet sand against the gusts of ocean wind.

Bridget's brother Teddy was slouched in one of the low-backed chairs. He and Bridget had both inherited the same elements of their parents' remarkable beauty: their mother's dark blue eyes, framed by their father's thick chestnut hair, which spilled over Bridget's shoulders in waves and hung over Teddy's brow in lush curls. Bridget complained frequently that Teddy's eyelashes were longer than hers, and his face was so pretty it sometimes seemed misplaced on a boy's shoulders. His long legs in their light summer flannels jutted out in front of him like the off-kilter framing beams of a half-finished building.

He took Clare in with a measuring glance that flickered over her face, dropped to her white cotton dress, and lingered on her bare arms.

Heat rushed into Clare's cheeks.

Bridget was thirteen, just a few months older than Clare. But Teddy was fifteen. In the men who orbited her mother, Clare sometimes caught glimpses of the boys they had once been: a child's excitement when they reported the speed of a new car, a boy's shyness when they tried to find the words to give a compliment. With Teddy, it was the opposite. She had met royalty who weren't as self-assured as him. But it wasn't the certainty of command. Teddy had no interest in getting anyone else to do anything, or much interest in what anyone else did at all, so long as it didn't interfere with him. So Clare knew that his long glance wasn't a greeting, or even a sign of curiosity: he was simply looking her over to see if he wanted anything.

Then he looked back at the ladies' magazine that lay open in his lap. Clare scanned the pages, upside down, as if they might tell her something. She was used to being invisible to Teddy. She didn't know what had caught his eye today. And she didn't know whether she liked it, or not.

The magazine contained a spread of flowers drawn in pen and ink, labeled according to their meaning.

"I don't know how you girls keep track of all this," he said. "It's more complicated than military code." He read down the list: "Roses, love. Mint, suspicion. Poppy, oblivion. Did you know all this, Bridget?"

"Aren't you going to sit down?" Bridget asked Clare.

Clare took the seat nearest to the door, on a low wicker couch opposite Teddy. Bridget sat beside her and wriggled down into the cushions with all the luxurious indolence of a favorite cat. "I'm so glad you're here," she told Clare. "Last week it felt like we were lost at sea."

Bridget and her family almost always arrived in a new town several days before anyone else. Bridget's mother liked to come ahead so that she could have the spiritual properties of their home inspected without attracting ignorant comment. And Bridget's father had frequently gotten involved in a misunderstanding with a young lady that made leaving their previous place expedient. But Bridget hated to be alone. She had told Clare once that if she sat too long in a room by herself, she began to worry if she even existed at all. For her, the long, quiet days before the rest of the crowd followed them to a new town were almost unendurable trials.

"Time moves so slow here, I keep wondering if it's

stopped," she went on. "Sometimes I think we're caught in a temporal anomaly."

"What's a temporal anomaly?" Clare asked.

Bridget loved to take the tone of an exasperated tutor, and she fell into it instantly now. "It's like a run in the fabric of time," she said. "And if you fall into it, you get left behind."

Clare had met several old women who still piled their hair in grotesque arrangements of braids and curls that her mother said had been the fashion in their youth, but this didn't seem to be exactly what Bridget meant. She tilted her head to think.

Dissatisfied with Clare's reaction, Bridget elaborated: "They eat boats."

Teddy slapped the magazine down on the table, still open to the article on the secret language of flowers. "Come on, Bridget," he said. "How do you tell a temporal anomaly from a shipwreck?"

Bridget sat up straight, her eyes glittering, not with true belief, but with delight at the prospect of battle.

"Does anyone ever escape from these temporal anomalies? To tell the tale?" Teddy prodded.

"Rip Van Winkle," Bridget retorted.

"Rip Van Winkle is a character in a book," Teddy said. "Not scientific evidence."

"But where do you learn all your science?" Bridget asked.

Her face twisted in triumph. "Oh, that's right!" she said. "*In a book.*"

Teddy stood.

"Where are you going?" Bridget demanded. "We're about to play truth or consequences."

Teddy shook his head. "The tide's almost out," he said. "I'm going down to the water."

He glanced at Clare, consulted the magazine on the table, then pulled a stem out of the arrangement: a waxy yellow bloom that Clare recognized as a buttercup. He presented it to her without comment, then straightened up, watching her like a boy who has just poked a frog and wants to see if it will jump.

Clare glared at him.

Teddy smiled faintly—to himself, not at her. Then he strode out of the room.

In an instant, Bridget had pounced on the magazine, her finger running down the names of the flowers. "What does it mean?" she said. "Which kind is it?"

"How should I know?" Clare said, and shoved it back among the rest.

FIVE

LARE'S MOTHER WAS THE one who found the key.

The day after she and Clare arrived, Clare's mother had risen before dawn: an involuntary habit which she lied about energetically, telling long rueful stories about her incurable laziness, complete with vivid descriptions of the way her dreams changed when she slept during daylight. If anyone insisted that he had caught a glimpse of her up on deck or disappearing down a country road in the early-morning hours, she insisted that he must be mistaken, or even imagining things. But every day, she continued to wake before sunrise, to the chime of some unknown clock.

That morning, dressed by dawn, she had walked out to the back garden, where she hadn't been able to resist cutting an armful of flowers with the pearl-handled knife she kept hidden in her pocket. She'd shaken the sleepy ants carefully from each blossom, then carried the bundle back up to the house. In Tilda's kitchen, she found the shelves arranged according to a system that was at once highly sophisticated and impossible to penetrate. Clare's mother hadn't been able to locate any suitable vases, and she was leery of Tilda's reaction if she simply dunked the stems in a cooking pot and left them in one of the pristine white sinks. At a loss, she had tiptoed back upstairs to her room, the bouquet still cradled in the crook of her arm.

There, to her delight, she had discovered a tall amber vase on top of the bookshelf. She filled it with water from her washroom sink and carefully arranged her conquests in it, creating a truly extraordinary bouquet in which almost every stem boasted a different bloom or shade, set off by half a dozen fronds of climbing rose, each fully three or four feet long, which arced over it all like the branches of a weeping willow. By this time, Clare was padding around her own room and the servants had begun to stir in the kitchen, so Clare's mother carried the arrangement back down the stairs to present to them at breakfast.

Tilda's eyes grew wide at the first sight of the heavy vase. Then she went mute with indignation. She served the breakfast with fierce efficiency, refusing to look at either Clare or her mother but occasionally taking furtive, anxious glances at Mack, like a nurse struggling to restrain her unbecoming concern for a favorite patient. Mack, already uneasy over Clare's mother's insistence that he share his breakfast with his employer and her daughter, tried gamely to make the appropriate compliments. But he couldn't refrain from stealing agonized glimpses at his plundered garden out the kitchen window.

"I can always cut a bouquet for you, Mrs. Fitzgerald," he told Clare's mother. "There's no need for you to bother."

This, of course, was not the reaction Clare's mother had in mind. But as always, her grasp of the situation was quick, and so were her adjustments. "Oh, I'd love that, Mack," she said. "You can see what a mess I've made here. I'm afraid I'm something of a savage."

Mack's eyes traveled over his brutalized sweet peas and lilies with the harried resignation of a farmer evaluating storm damage. He didn't contradict her.

For the rest of the meal, whenever Mack found himself forced by politeness to meet Clare's mother's eyes, she gave him a nonsensically bright smile. By this, Clare knew that her mother was unhappy. A few years before, Clare might have spent the whole meal inventing compliments to make up for the ones Mack hadn't made, or offered her mother bits of toast dragged in marmalade or bacon grease. When this failed, Clare would have used up the rest of the morning imagining more clever things she might have said, or better temptations she might have offered: all for nothing. The campaigns she had waged in the past to ease her mother's sorrows had all been a waste, if they hadn't made things worse. By now she knew the best thing to do was leave her mother be.

As soon as the meal was done, Clare's mother carried the bouquet back up to her own room, where she refused to allow Tilda to cull or freshen it for a week.

"They don't have to be perfect to keep," she told Tilda, at Tilda's first attempt to remove several spent lilies on her morning patrol of the room. "Leave them for a day."

When Tilda returned the next morning, determination shining on her face, Clare's mother again stopped her with a word. "Oh, you'd better leave them, Tilda," she said. "I like to see how they change when they fade."

Thwarted for the second time, Tilda obeyed with a vengeance: over the following days, as the stems drooped and the water in the vase turned to thick milk, she ignored the bouquet completely. She even neglected to wipe up the gold pollen that fell on the slick wood of the bedside table where the vase stood.

By the end of the week, the leaves of the trailing rose branches had turned gray-green and brittle. The small pink roses had folded, and their petals dropped to the floor in clouds at the vibration from any step. Half the color had drained from the splayed petals of the tulips, and the blue delphinium had gone almost black. The smell of sweet rot filled the room even when the windows were wide open.

"Do you want me to take care of them?" Clare finally asked. She had come to see if her mother was ready to go down for breakfast, but stopped in the doorway at the strong scent.

Her mother, arrayed in the seemingly infinite folds of a white chiffon dressing gown, her blond hair unbound and gleaming in the early sun, looked up from the wing chair by the window, where she was curled up with a history of Rome. She had discovered it on the bookshelf and had been terrifying her conversational partners with it all week, introducing crucifixions and regicide to the conversation with barely concealed glee whenever the topic turned to the popular novels or sentimental poetry her friends liked to read. Her friends, of course, were both fascinated and appalled. They couldn't work up any indignation against a diseased imagination, since the events had actually happened, and they could hardly dismiss the history of the empire as a tawdry scandal, so after a few false starts they had begun to object to her comments on the basis of good taste: the world was full of true stories, they agreed, but simple truth hardly made a thing worth repeating. This charge allowed them to retell the gory tales, as evidence in the case against Clare's mother, both endlessly and with impunity.

"Oh, sweetheart," Clare's mother said. "Does it bother you? I'll take care of them right now."

In a rush of chiffon, she rose, swept up the amber vase and its contents, and carried it into her bathroom. A trail of pollen mixed with dropped petals marked her way. Clare knelt and collected the stray petals from the carpet, then followed.

Her mother had already shoved the remains of the bouquet face-down into the starched white case that lined the wicker wastebasket. Gray-green stains spread into the crisp fabric like watercolor blooming on rag paper. Foul water poured from the lip of the vase into the sink in a steady stream.

Then, as the stream subsided, something clinked inside the amber glass.

"What's that?" Clare asked.

Clare's mother turned the faucet on, ran clean water into the vase, and swirled it around. Then she turned the entire vase upside down.

A small key fell out, bleeding rust into the white sink.

"What do you suppose this is for?" Clare's mother asked, and retrieved it.

Clare knew instantly. The handle of the key was a fili-gree leaf, its veins described by mottled green metal. The oxidized copper matched the bones of the glass house, and the veins of the leaf followed the same weird patterns as the etching on its door. She didn't answer.

Downstairs at breakfast, Clare's mother laid the key be-side her plate as Tilda set a glass of orange juice down at her place.

"Where did you get that?" Tilda asked, her voice sharp with surprise.

"We found it," Clare's mother said. "At the bottom of a vase."

Her satisfaction at having rattled Tilda was cut short by Tilda's confiscation of the key. One moment it lay on the table. The next it had disappeared into one of the capacious pockets of Tilda's apron.

Now it was Clare's mother's voice that rose in surprise. "Does it go to something, then?" she asked.

"The glass house," Tilda told her.

"The glass house?" Clare's mother repeated. "Is it locked?"

Tilda gave a resolute nod.

Clare's mother held her hand out, palm up. "Well, I'm sure we'd love to have the key to it. It looks like a perfect little jewel."

"We don't use the glass house," Tilda told her. "Not for years."

Clare's mother lifted her hand higher. "I'm sure we would."

In answer, Tilda walked to a drawer in the far corner of the kitchen, opened it, and dropped the key in.

Before lunch, Clare had stolen it.

Six

STEALING THE KEY WAS child's play.

Every morning after breakfast, Tilda made her rounds of the house with a bark basket of cleaning supplies: lemon oil, bleached rags, and a duster that appeared to be handmade from the green and black feathers of several fancy local chickens.

After Clare's mother retreated to her own room, where she usually spent the morning with some book, Clare took up a sentry position at the top of the stairs. She waited until Tilda crossed the dining room below and listened as her footsteps faded into the far reaches of the house. Then Clare slipped down to the kitchen. The key was just where Tilda had left it, nestled on a pile of striped dishtowels. An instant later, Clare had hidden it snugly in the sash of her dress.

The whole operation had gone so fast and been so simple that she actually felt a little disappointed. But to get to the glass house without attracting attention was a different challenge.

Clare surveyed the yard through the windows over the garden. The glade of maples around the glass house and the vines that grew over it made the interior invisible from the big house. Once she reached it, she'd be hidden. But if she approached it directly, down the slope of the back lawn, anybody could see her from any of the back windows. The only concealed approach was through the forest that bounded the backyard and made a sloppy triangle with the road that ran away from the property. The glass house sat in the crook of this triangle. If she cut through the woods, they would screen her until she reached it.

Clare slipped out the kitchen door onto the pebble drive. She loitered along it, feigning interest in the cracked shells among the small gray stones, until it brought her within a few feet of the forest. Then she darted into the trees.

She was surprised by the sudden chill under the canopy. The early-summer sun had warmed the broad lawn but not the green shadows of the forest. She was used to the manicured shade and well-behaved trees of city gardens, but here thick underbrush grew between the big trunks. She couldn't take a single step without stopping to think where to put her foot next. And the place was haunted by sounds. Unseen creatures lurked in the brambles until she was almost upon them, then exploded, still invisible, through the brush. Startled birds swooped from their perches, cawing alarms. Before she reached the glass house she was as jumpy as a fawn, and when she finally caught sight of it, she lunged out of the woods like an animal breaking cover.

On the mossy flagstone by the door, the fright began to drain from her. She pulled the key from her sash. It settled cleanly into the lock. She turned it, stepped inside, replaced the key at her waist, and pulled the door shut behind her.

A book dropped to the floor with the unmistakable rattle of pages falling together.

Clare caught her breath and scanned the room.

A few dozen titles were stacked in crooked piles on the buffet, between the mismatched candelabras. But the sound hadn't come from there.

It had come from the center of the room, near the divan.

The divan, sea-foam green, formed a half moon along with a pair of mulberry wing chairs that stood at opposite ends of a low table with a single shallow drawer. Clare slipped past the hulk of the piano and stepped by one of the wing chairs, into the ring. A book had fallen to the richly patterned rug beside the divan, face-down, its boards splayed, its gilt-edged pages curled.

Instinctively, Clare bent down to pick it up and set it right. But before her outstretched hand touched the cover, the book rose from the rug, by the spine, until its boards and pages hung straight. Then it toppled over on its side.

Clare straightened up.

The book lay flat and still.

Clare stared fiercely. She knew the power of her imagination. It had created angel after angel to stand guard outside lonely hotel rooms. It had invented whole civilizations in the darkness beyond the windows of speeding night trains. But until this moment, she had never had any trouble telling the difference between the products of her imagination and the actual world.

Her mind called back the new memory of the falling book, to see if it worked differently than other memories. She remembered stepping through the door, the sudden sound, the book's slow rise from the floor. Then she played it back again. But the memory was too fresh for this kind of treatment. Each time she tried to go over it, the ceiling of the glass house in her mind grew higher and higher until it towered several stories overhead. The furniture multiplied and divided. The imaginary book changed color in her mind from simple brown, to green, to red.

Frustrated, Clare stooped to pick up the real book. *Hawthorne* was printed on the dull brown spine in gold letters. She flipped the cover open to the title page: *Mosses from an Old Manse.*

Beside her, someone sighed.

The sigh came from nearby, close enough that it sounded like the person who gave it could reach out and touch her. But no one stood where the sound had come from. And before her mind could work out this problem, she caught sight of Tilda not ten yards away, just beyond the glade, carrying an armful of peonies up to the big house as if they were a basket of unwashed laundry.

Clare dropped to her knees. An instant later, she was spread-eagled on the rug, out of the old woman's line of sight, the book under her belly.

She lay like that, her forehead pressed into the rough carpet, until her heart stopped pounding. Then she lay there a while longer. She had just started to calculate whether Tilda had made it back up to the big house or not when a light hand touched her shoulder.

"Are you all right?" a boy's voice asked.

Clare sprang upright. She scrambled back on the rug until her shoulders struck the divan.

No one was in sight.

Clare glanced outside. Tilda was gone. The lawn was empty.

As she scanned the glass house again, Clare's eyes narrowed. She hated to be the victim of a trick.

"Who's there?" she demanded.

Her skin tingled with fear, but her curiosity was stronger. Gingerly, she stood. She checked behind the divan, circled the wing chairs, peered under the lid of the piano.

"I'm sorry," the voice said.

Clare froze in the shadow of the piano's wing.

"I didn't mean to scare you," the voice added. It wasn't a child's voice, and it wasn't a man's. It belonged to a boy her age, or maybe a bit older. And it still came from the same spot near the divan, where no one stood.

"Who's there?" Clare repeated.

The silence lasted so long that Clare began to wonder again if the whole episode had been a trick of her own mind. Then the voice answered from the piano bench, just a few steps away: "Jack."

"Jack who?" Clare asked.

Another silence. Then, "Cunningham."

Seemingly of its own accord, the piano played the first few notes of a simple melody. Clare shuddered.

"Stop it!" she said.

The melody broke off.

"You don't like that song?" Jack asked, surprised.

"Who are you?" Clare demanded again.

In the silence that followed, she realized how much trouble she would have had answering that question once she'd already told someone her name. And something else: how little a name actually told you about anyone.

Jack seemed stymied by the same problem. "I live here," he said finally.

"In the glass house?" Clare asked.

"And the lawn," he said. "And the woods."

"What about the big house?"

Jack fell silent again. The stillness broke the spell his voice had cast. Doubt crept over Clare again. Had she fallen asleep without realizing? Had her other daydreams ever been this vivid?

"Jack?" she asked.

"I don't go up there," he said.

"Why not?"

"Where do you live?" he asked.

This was another question that should have a simple answer, and didn't. "I just came down from the house," Clare said.

"I saw you come," he said impatiently. "That's not what I meant."

Clare named the town on the coast of France where she and her mother had spent the winter.

"You're not French," he said immediately, as if she'd just offered some absurd bluff in a game of cards.

"No," Clare admitted.

His limited patience had thinned to exasperation. "You have a house somewhere, don't you?" he said. "Where is it?"

Clare folded her arms over her belly. "We haven't been there in three years," she said.

"Three years?" he repeated. She didn't need to see his face to guess his thoughts. She could hear the disbelief in his voice.

Clare nodded.

A few days after Clare's father's funeral, Clare's mother had announced their first excursion. She had bought a pair of tickets for a private car on the transatlantic railroad between New York and California, to clear their heads, she said. But the miles of wild land and the sheer size of the mountains, which until then she had never seen, only intensified her sense that she and her daughter were now alone in a vast and perhaps unfriendly universe. Clare woke several times in the dead of night to find her mother still clothed, staring out the train window at the indecipherable stars. "I can't decide if they want to tell us something," she said. "Or if we should know better than to ask just by looking at them." In any case, Clare's mother concluded, the trip had hardly been a rest. So the day after they returned home she announced their next, this time to celebrate the Italian *carnevale* in Viareggio.

For several months after that, they hadn't spent more than two days home at a stretch. Every return was followed by the almost immediate discovery of another boat about to leave port, another treasure Clare had to see, another distant festival. And after all, her mother would observe brightly, their things were already packed. It was almost easier to go on another trip than it would be to put them all back.

Then, less than six months after Clare's father died, Clare's mother rented out the house where Clare had grown up on a permanent basis. This wasn't from financial necessity, but over an incident with a maid.

Clare and her mother had come into town that night on a nine o'clock train. It was late summer, fully two weeks before the great autumn migration would bring most of their friends back from the coast to the city. Her mother was already in a wild mood. She had packed all their things without warning the night before, then woken Clare at dawn to declare that they were leaving on the next train. Clare hadn't even bothered to search her memory for a reason for the rush. It could have been a slight from a friend or a shipwrecked flirtation, but more likely the impulse to escape came from a change in the secret weather of her mother's mind. Her mother could sail impervious through reversals and snubs that would have sunk another woman. But she was defenseless against her own thoughts. Sleepily, Clare had dressed in the clothes her mother had saved out for her, and submitted to the journey. At first it hadn't seemed like an emergency: they were constantly leaving places before the end of a season, and everyone else would follow them back to the city in a matter of weeks.

But the maid who answered their ring that evening made a serious tactical error. She told Clare's mother that getting their tower of luggage up the front steps was impossible.

"I'm the only one here, ma'am," she explained. "Albert's already out to the bar, and he won't come back till two or three."

"Impossible?" Clare's mother repeated, as if taking offense at some ugly word shouted at her in the street.

The maid nodded back at her with the faintest trace of defiance.

Clare's mother marched back down the steps. Using a bag of gold coins she traveled with solely for their dramatic effect at moments like this, she hired four porters in as many minutes: a pair of boys in short pants who were loitering by the gate to the park across the street, a young man she commandeered from a walk with his sweetheart, and an older gentleman who gave Clare's mother a long mooning glance each time he carried a trunk up the steps. Ten minutes later, all the trunks and boxes were stacked neatly inside the door of their front hall. When Clare's mother had released her temporary servants back to the four winds, she turned to the maid.

"I could have gotten better service than this," Clare's mother told her, "at the worst hotel in town." She picked up the phone by the door and placed a call. Five minutes later, a pair of drivers from the private force employed by one of the city's best hotels had carried all their luggage back down. It was the last time Clare set foot inside her own house.

"It's not as though we've really lived there for years," her mother told her when she announced her decision to rent it out. "Now you can order peach flambé for breakfast every morning."

Clare loved the peach flambé they served at fine restaurants. She liked the salt air that blew through rented seaside rooms. She liked hotel vases full of tulips that changed like magic to daffodils while she was out. She liked the bellmen at the doors with their pockets full of mints. She liked the sound of rain on the roof of a cab, and the lavender they used to scent linens in Paris. She couldn't explain to her mother why she preferred her own room, which had only one window and was still furnished with the fading chintz of her childhood, to any of this. And because she couldn't find the words, she didn't say anything.

Now the boy's voice was incredulous. "Then where do you live?" he asked.

Automatically, Clare adopted the pose of world-weary sophistication that usually silenced other children who asked the same questions. "All over," she said. "We get whatever rooms we want for the season."

By the big house, Clare caught a flash of motion. She glanced up. Tilda strode across the lawn, her apron blazing in the sun. Her destination was unmistakable: the glass house.

Clare darted around the piano to the door.

"What's wrong?" Jack demanded.

"Tilda," Clare whispered.

Jack laughed and Clare caught a hint of the horror that sound could conjure if it rang without explanation through the glass house. "She won't hurt you," he said. "She comes to hear me play."

"She comes here?" Clare repeated, at the door now. She pushed it open and stepped out onto the mossy flagstone.

"Wait!" Jack said. "Will you come back?"

Tilda had almost reached the glade.

Clare swung the door shut, locked it, and leapt over the small span of lawn into the shelter of the woods. She crashed through them for a few breathless moments, then emerged a good twenty feet from the glass house, waving.

Beside the glass house, Tilda drew up short.

"Hello!" Clare called. "I've been for a ramble!"

Tilda's eyes narrowed. She peered through the etching on the glass house door, then tried the handle. It held fast.

Clare tramped through the grass between them. "It's locked," she said helpfully. "I tried it the other day."

Tilda stared straight into Clare's eyes, measuring her not with the quick glance most adults gave to children, but closely, as if Clare were already a grown woman. Her steady gaze filled Clare with unease. But it also gave her a strange sense of satisfaction.

"The key is missing again," Tilda said. "Do you have it?"

SEVEN

"HE KEY?" CLARE SAID. "It's not in the drawer? Are you sure?"

Without waiting for Tilda's answer, she set off across the lawn.

Tilda followed, matching Clare's brisk pace step for step until they came around the side of the house to the kitchen door. Then Clare shot ahead, flying up the short flight of stairs into the house. Before Tilda had even reached the threshold, Clare had gotten the drawer open and dropped the key back in.

Behind her, paper rattled.

She whirled around.

Mack sat at the small table by the window, his smile wry over the top fold of a crisp newspaper.

Before Clare could decide whether he'd caught her or not, Tilda burst through the door.

"Look!" Clare said brightly. She pointed to the key,

which had fallen on a worn white towel, underlined by a thin blue stripe. "I found it!"

Tilda glared at the key. Then she appealed to Mack. "That wasn't here before," she said darkly.

"Maybe it got pushed to the back," Clare said. "Or hidden under something."

Mack gave a noncommittal shrug and took refuge behind his columns of newsprint.

Tilda gave Clare another measuring look. Then she picked the key up, dropped it in her pocket, and swatted the drawer shut.

In the week since they'd arrived, Clare had made no progress in cracking Tilda's stony façade. Clare's mother's skirmishes with the maid hadn't helped. And this was hardly how Clare would have chosen to advance her campaign to win her way into Tilda's good graces. But Clare had long practice in keeping her composure through emergencies far more troubling than this. She didn't bat an eye.

Tilda stalked over to the icebox. She pulled out a piece of beef and a small bowl of hard-boiled eggs and set them on the counter beside a loaf of bread and a bunch of greens.

With deft strokes, Tilda sawed off several thin, perfect slices of bread. "Can I make you something?" she asked Mack. "Egg sandwich? Beef with gravy?"

He shook his head and pushed his crumb-strewn plate forward. "I got something already," he said.

Even if Mack had seen her with the key, Clare calculated, he would have given her up by now if he was going to. And she wasn't about to leave the kitchen without discovering where the key was laid to rest next. She took the seat at the window opposite Mack.

"Have you worked here a long time?" she asked. This was another reliable question with servants: if they liked their place, they could go on about their history. And if they didn't, it was a chance for them to talk about anyplace else they'd ever been, or anywhere else they dreamed of going.

Mack let his paper drop just low enough that she could see his eyes. He gave an amiable nod. Then he raised the paper again.

But Clare knew she was still young enough to be permitted a child's steady stream of questions. "How long?" she pressed.

"Fifty years," Mack said, from beyond the paper.

"Forty-eight," said Tilda.

Clare glanced at Tilda, trying to mask her own surprise. All her other attempts to draw Tilda out since they arrived had failed. Clare hadn't expected to lure her into this conversation at all, especially not over a detail so small.

Mack let his paper drop again. His brow furrowed as he calculated. "I guess so," he said.

"They hired us both the summer they built the place," Tilda said, with a note of reproach, like a woman who has to remind a man of some promise he made.

"Who?" Clare asked.

It wasn't a hard question, or an impolite one, but it seemed to surprise Tilda. She looked at Mack.

"They're gone now," Mack said. "God rest."

Clare's eyebrows rose. It wasn't unusual for servants to welcome guests to a rented house. But she'd never heard of them staying at a place past the owner's death.

"Then who do we rent from?" she asked.

Mack finally capitulated. He folded his paper and laid it beside his plate. "The new man," he said. "It was too much trouble for him to find other help when he bought the house, so he just kept us on." His eyes crinkled in a smile. "Which was good for us. Because after forty-eight years, I'm not sure we're much good for anything else."

Mack's smile made Clare bold.

"What about the boy," she tried, "who lived in the room upstairs?"

Tilda's knife rattled on the counter.

Mack's smile flickered. Then it turned teasing. "Wouldn't

you rather hear about the boys who live around here now?"
he asked.

Now it was Clare's turn to descend into confusion.
She'd spent years studying the people she met, learning their
habits, sorting them by type. But now that she was an expert
at being a child, they wanted her to become something else.
And suddenly, that was all anyone wanted to talk with her
about.

"There's time enough for that," Tilda said, her voice
sharp.

Clare turned to her, startled. She'd never heard a hint of
harshness in Tilda's voice when she spoke to Mack before.
And she didn't know if Tilda had meant to defend her or
not. But she felt a wave of gratitude.

Tilda sliced decisively through the sandwich she had
made, lifted the pieces onto a plate with the flat of her knife,
and put the plate on a painted tray. Then she picked up the
tray and carried it out the door, the key still in her pocket.

Clare scrambled down from her chair, nodded a hasty
goodbye to Mack, and followed.

Tilda had already left the dining room when Clare
reached it. She couldn't have had time to dispose of the key
there. Careful to keep out of sight, Clare darted to the hall,
listened as Tilda mounted the stairs, then crept halfway up
them herself.

Overhead, Tilda crossed the landing. Clare's mother's voice drifted down from above. "Oh, Tilda, thank you," she said. "You're just like an angel from heaven. All you need is a flaming sword to complete the effect."

Tilda didn't dignify this greeting with a response. Dishes and silver clinked. Linen sighed. Tilda lingered in Clare's mother's room so long that Clare began to worry that she had chosen a new hiding spot for the key there. Then Clare came to her senses: Tilda would never risk leaving it any-place where it might fall into Clare's mother's clutches again.

Silently, Clare ascended the rest of the flight. At the top, the door to the boy's room stood open. She ducked inside and slipped behind it. Through the crack at the hinge she commanded a view of the entire landing and a glimpse of her mother's room. When Tilda emerged, Clare would be able to see her every move.

But when Tilda came out onto the landing a few minutes later, she was empty-handed. She paused for a breath or two. Then she made straight for the boy's room.

Behind the door, Clare shrank back. Her mind filled with excuses, all of them absurd: she'd thought she heard someone singing back there, she'd forgotten which room was hers. But Tilda strode right past the door that concealed Clare, into the room.

Very slowly, as if afraid her head might creak on her neck, Clare turned to see what Tilda was doing.

Tilda stood with her back to Clare, one hand closed on something in her apron pocket. She looked over the tidy bed, the dresser, the pair of mirrors that multiplied without end. Then she went to the desk, pulled open a drawer, and dropped something in.

Clare held her breath, still hidden behind the door as Tilda passed by for the second time. But the old woman stepped back out into the hall without detecting Clare.

She remained stock-still as Tilda retreated down the stairs. When she heard her turn for the kitchen, Clare slipped from behind the door and went to the desk.

The first drawer she opened was filled with feathers: white, downy gray, brown on a yellow stalk, blue jay. She pushed them aside to reveal a dozen loose green marbles and a large clear red shooter. The shallow center drawer contained school papers of some kind: several thin notebooks, a speller, and a book of figures, along with a handful of rock-hard caramels wrapped in yellowed wax paper. In the next drawer she found a short blue cut-glass tumbler with a chipped lip in which someone had collected iron nails along with a small battalion of toy soldiers. When Clare looked closer, she realized that all of the figures had been marred as they were poured. Each of them was missing an arm, or a leg, or some feature: a hollow where their eyes should have been, a smooth metal plane instead of lips. The key had fallen among them so that a bayonet protruded through its filigree handle.

Clare pulled the key free and dropped it into her own pocket. Then she set off in search of a candle and a bar of soap.

This was another technique gleaned from the ship's detective. Soap, he had told her mother, would take the impression of a simple key, and the impression could then serve as a mold to make a duplicate key of molten wax.

Clare found the soap in the bathroom she shared with her mother, and discovered a supply of candles in a clandestine search of the dining room buffet.

But like many of the criminal techniques the ship's detective had learned about in books, this one presented a number of real-life challenges that the authors had apparently failed to mention. When Clare made her first attempt, at the desk in her own room, the bar of stolen soap wouldn't take any impression at all. And when Clare pressed with all her strength, it just crumbled into flakes. A more expensive bar, with spikes of lavender suspended in glycerin, finally took the imprint of one side of the key. Then Clare had to go looking for another soap to complete the mold, depleting her mother's stash almost completely with the theft of a bar laced with orange and mint.

When she was satisfied that the mirror images in the soap would serve to make an accurate copy of the key, Clare turned to the candles. Her first attempt to dribble wax into the mold resulted in a singed lump shot through with traces of the pink dye that colored the candle. It looked more like some sea creature washed up on the beach than a key. But gradually she refined her technique until she could drop the hot wax evenly, first into the teeth of the key, then down the long stem, and finally into the handle. After a few more tries, she lifted the lavender soap away to reveal a piece of wax that was almost an exact match to its metal cousin on the desk. The filigree of the handle hadn't survived the transfer. The whorls and veins in the copper leaf had melted into one thick mass. But other than that, it was perfect. Clare blew gently on the wax as it turned from translucent to milky. Then she freed it from the mold with the tip of a sharp pencil. The wax was light, but pleasingly solid.

She slipped the new key into her pocket and regarded the evidence she'd created: the half-burnt tapers, the imprinted soap. The tapers were easily explained by a fear of the dark, but the soap was a dead giveaway. And it was impossible to hide things in a house with a maid. She pushed the desk aside so she could get to the window, opened it, and looked down. Below, a thick cover of narcissus grew right up to the whitewashed brick of the exterior wall. Clare did a quick check to be sure no one was in the yard, then let the bars of soap drop past the dining room window into the long leaves of the paper whites. A few of the blooms trembled from the impact. Then the garden was still.

Clare closed the window and laid the tapers in a drawer. She trailed silently around the landing to the boy's room, where she settled the original key back among the tin men. Then she went out, her hand closed around the new key in her pocket.

EIGHT

THE OCEAN NEVER STOPS," Bridget complained, staring out at the dark surf beyond the circle of light from the fire they'd built on the beach. "Not even when the sun goes down. It's like some awful machine that works all night and doesn't make anything."

"You've suffered so much," Teddy said. "I don't know how you bear it."

Bridget kicked sand in his direction, but her aim was compromised by her extreme slouch in the wooden chair. The sand landed in the fire between them. The flames guttered, then blazed up again. Clare glanced at the dark sea. All along the water's edge, paper lanterns hung between poles anchored in the wet sand. The poles were about the height of a man, so the party guests had to duck under them to reach the surf, where colored light reflected on the water between washes of white foam.

A few guests lingered at the shoreline. Most of them milled around linen-covered buffet tables surrounded by another lazy square of lanterns a safe distance from the tide. But the five young people had dragged their chairs down the beach and lit a fire of their own.

This had been Denby's idea. He and Bram had only arrived that afternoon, but as usual Denby had already taken charge of everything. For her part, Clare had been glad to leave the general party. Bridget's father had taken a marked interest in Clare's mother that evening, and instead of putting him off, Clare's mother had embarked with him on an intense conversation. When Clare noticed the glances cast in their direction she had begun to loiter nearby, but her presence hadn't interrupted the discussion, which at that point centered on sea monsters. Her mother played the skeptic, but Bridget's father insisted there must be creatures so rare or shy that they'd escaped mankind. He was also unwilling to concede the possibility of mermaids. In fact, he said, he'd rather not live in a world where it could be proved that they did not exist. When Bridget had come to collect Clare, Clare hadn't objected.

On the other side of the fire, Bram glanced at Denby.

"We could take them to the cave," he said.

Denby raised his eyebrows, considering.

"What cave?" Bridget asked.

Bram and Denby's eyes locked in a silence that conveyed the strong impression that they had learned somewhere to communicate using only their minds. From the time they could walk, the two boys, born less than a month apart, had been almost inseparable, a situation that had become permanent after Bram's mother died the summer he turned seven. By the time Bram's father emerged from his fog of grief, he discovered that Denby had established a cot for Bram in his room and claimed a sailor's hammock in Bram's room for himself. These arrangements were only minor tactical moves in pursuit of Denby's main object, which was that the two boys should spend no waking hour apart. Denby's father, a universally feared sugar magnate whose far-flung business concerns kept him on a seemingly endless circuit of the globe, offered no objection. Neither did Denby's mother, who smiled so rarely that it was a topic of discussion whether she didn't think the jokes she heard were funny or didn't realize they were jokes. And after his wife's death, Bram's father found it almost impossible to refuse his son anything.

From that point on, Bram and Denby were the terror and pride of their set. They smeared cats with jam and tied jewelry to the tails of patient dogs. They eluded their maids on outings and returned home hours later, their faces black with soot, their hair adorned with goose feathers. Because everyone was secretly pleased to see that good blood hadn't run too thin to boil yet, they became a favorite topic of conversation, their exploits inflated over countless retellings. A stray dog they'd tamed became a lion cub. A tutor who had fallen victim to their pranks was promoted to ambassador from France.

The boys were both fourteen this summer, two years older than Clare, a year older than Bridget, but a year younger than Teddy. Denby, tall, pale, with angular features and a mop of straight brown hair, was the clear leader. He conceived the plans, but Bram made them happen. Handsome, with clear blue eyes and sandy curls, Bram was always the first to scale a tree or hop a fence, then reached back to pull the others up. He had been Bridget's crush since the previous summer, but so far her determined flirting had yielded inconclusive results.

"There's a cave on the water," Denby announced. "Under the bluff."

Most of the summer homes were built on the rise above the beach. But north along the shore a few of the homes, including the one Denby's family had taken that summer, sat on a stone cliff that dropped directly into the sea.

"It's the biggest cave I've ever seen," Denby went on. "We could only go so far without a torch. But we didn't find the end of it."

Clare wondered what artifacts the local gossip would furnish the cave with by the end of the summer: a trove of pirate treasure, a set of human bones.

"You couldn't have found it under the bluff," Teddy objected. "The surf would break you up on the rocks."

"Not when the tide goes out," Denby countered.

"The tide's out now," said Teddy.

Suddenly, all three boys were on their feet. Bram gave a whoop and sprinted away across the sand. Teddy stooped to retrieve the box of matches and a branch of driftwood. Denby looked down at Bridget.

"Well?" he said. "Are you coming?"

The five of them straggled north along the beach. The back of Clare's neck prickled, but she didn't know if it was from fear of the dark ahead, or from fear they'd be caught before they escaped into it. But all five of them passed through the swirl of the party and back into the night without attracting a single comment.

When they passed the last light, Clare put her hand in her pocket. It closed on the stem of the key she had copied that afternoon. The handle was a clumsy blob, but the key itself was blunt and perfect.

"There's no cave," Teddy called through the darkness. "You've brought us out here to sell us to pirates."

"They wouldn't take you," Denby retorted. "Your father isn't rich enough."

The stripe of beach narrowed. Overhead, the grassy rise

gave way to the soaring stone of the bluff. Then the sand ran out at a jumble of large black rocks, still shining with seawater from the tide that had gone out. The surf lapped at the damp sand a dozen feet off.

Ahead of them, on the last slip of dry beach, Bram kicked off his shoes and socks. Then he struck out across the wet sand, leaving deep prints that filled immediately with dark water, until the bluff seemed to swallow him up.

When the rest of them reached the spot where Bram had stopped, Teddy and Denby shed their shoes and socks as well. Teddy bent to roll up his trousers while Bridget and Clare fumbled with the clasps of their sandals. Then, single file, they followed in Bram's tracks across the sand.

As they came around the curve of the bluff, the dark mouth of a cave yawned in the sheer rock. A long finger of the tide cut a channel into its hidden depths. The dimensions were hard to make out in the dark, but to Clare the cave looked to be about as wide as a three-car garage and high enough for a small sailboat to pass into without dropping its mast. Bram was already clambering over chunks of the bluff that had fallen into the sea, which were so jagged and slick that as the rest of them ventured after Bram, even Teddy hesitated, looking for the next sure step. Clare and Bridget clung together, steadying each other as they crept barefoot from rock to rock. But finally the four of them clustered at the lip of the cave on a narrow ledge that ran along the black water back into darkness.

"Hang on," Teddy said as Denby took his first step into the cave. Wood rattled inside cardboard. Then Teddy struck a match to reveal one of his argyle socks wrapped around the stick of driftwood he'd carried down the beach. He held the flame to the blue and white knit. When it caught and flared, a terrible keening wail split the darkness.

Denby staggered back into the girls. Bridget clutched Clare's arm. Teddy thrust his torch forward.

Laughter echoed through the cave. A minute later, Bram emerged from the shadows, his face red with torchlight. "Denby," he said, breathless with glee. "You should see your face."

"You sounded just like a ghost," Bridget said, and touched Bram's arm. "I was so scared."

"Ghosts aren't real," Denby snapped.

"Yes, they are," Teddy said. Then he added, with a victor's scorn: "But they're dead."

To reclaim his authority, Denby snatched the torch from Teddy and set off along the ledge, leaving the rest of them in deepening shadow. Bram sprang after him. Bridget trailed after Bram. Clare followed Bridget, with Teddy bringing up the rear.

As they pressed deeper into the cave, the low ceiling rose and the channel from the sea opened into a black pond that rocked gently against its stone banks with each pull of the tide. Over it, the rough walls leapt up to a domed ceiling several stories high, like the atrium of a fine hotel. When they reached the far bank of the pond, the ledge gave out onto uneven gray stones.

Denby hesitated.

"Go ahead," Bram said. "We got farther than this before."

"I don't know about that," Denby said.

"Yeah," Bram insisted. "I couldn't see the sun then, but I can still see the moon from here."

Clare glanced back. The glimmer of light was faint but clear on the ocean beyond.

"Follow the wall," Bram said. "That's all we did last time."

Denby set off again, reluctant, his upraised palm brushing the stone beside him. A few steps later, they came to the turn that Bram and Denby must have taken on their earlier visit: a slit in the stone, perhaps half as wide as a proper door. Denby raised the torch, but all it revealed was a cramped passage, not what lay beyond.

"That's it!" Bram exclaimed. "Where does it go?" He scrambled over the rocks and craned his neck to see in.

Not to be outdone, Denby pushed past him into the passage. Bram dove after. Bridget followed Bram. The light of the torch vanished with them.

Teddy brushed past Clare, but she didn't budge. She wouldn't have hesitated on the threshold of the world's finest hotel, but the cave was so dark and strange that she had no way to guess what might happen next—and so she couldn't act. She couldn't bring herself to step through the stone gap. She couldn't imagine walking back down the ledge to the beach on her own. And if she waited any longer, she'd be left in the dark by the pond, alone.

In the stone gap, Teddy turned back. He held out his hand. "Clare," he said.

She took it and followed him.

The passage proved to be little more than a few steps, a sharp turn, and a few more steps. Then it let out into a giant cavern. This ceiling was even higher than the one over the pond, festooned with pale tapered columns of rock that dropped down from the ceiling like the pendants of a gigantic chandelier. Below them, the floor was covered with the same weird white stone, but on the ground it lay in overlapping pools, like wax that had dropped from huge candles far above.

In the center of the room, Denby held the torch up, over his head. Bram was halfway across it, catching up to him. Bridget gamely picked her way along behind them. Clare tried to pull her hand from Teddy's, but he slid his arm around her waist. His lips found her face just under her eye.

Clare's skin crawled as if a spider had just run over it. She yanked free. But inside she had another feeling, as if warm caramel had just spilled in her rib cage.

At the sound, Denby turned.

"Hey!" he shouted. "What are you two doing?"

"Nothing," Teddy called as he strode forward. "Clare's just getting used to the dark, is all."

NINE

CLARE GLANCED AROUND THE glass house, looking for a heat shimmer or a stray shadow that
might give Jack away.

No books sailed from the buffet. No trinkets levitated
from their place.

In the few days since she made the wax key, Clare had
carried it with her everywhere she went. But this was the
first time she had returned to the glass house with it.

Despite the civilized veneer of Bridget's mother's mediums, Clare had never been able to forget the fact that ghosts
were dead. They had something to do with the stench of
jellyfish rotting on sand, and the glossy coffin that held her
father underground. It wasn't that she was afraid of death.
The loss of her father had robbed death of its mystery. She
knew how it looked and felt, so it could no longer terrorize
her the way it did other children. But she didn't want to
share it.

Her father had never returned to talk with her the way

Jack talked to her. Despite all the times she'd longed for him, she'd never felt her father's presence as she walked down another lonely hall or tried to will herself to sleep on another speeding train. But death was where she would find him again, a secret world that belonged only to the two of them. It had become a retreat for her: an escape and a shelter like the glass house, where she and her father could watch the world go by with all the sound cut off.

So to speak with someone from the other side now carried the threat of truth. It reminded her that death was not her private retreat, but everyone's common fate, vast and unknown, like the moment she'd been left in the cave alone, multiplied forever.

Several days had passed before her curiosity about Jack had overcome her reluctance to face this. On the way down the hill, she'd steeled herself against fear, and braced for a prank.

But the thought that she might return to find Jack gone had never crossed her mind.

She folded her arms against a wave of disappointment. Wind in the leaves above made the shadows on the furniture ripple like shallows at the water's edge. Jack hadn't terrified her when he was there, but now that he was gone, the glass house seemed truly haunted by the other world where he belonged.

She went over to the divan and sat down.

Before her father's death, on some Sunday mornings, they had crossed the park their house stood on to visit the small stone church on the other side. Among the garble of ideas Clare collected there, she had gleaned that God knew everything. This made her cautious. Life, as far as she could tell, was an elaborate dance that turned on knowing when to tell the truth and when to keep it secret. In her experience, the truth could only be tolerated sparingly. If people knew what she thought of them, or if she actually did whatever she wanted, she and her mother would never be invited anywhere again. So if God knew all these things, could he be trusted to keep them secret? More important, what must he think? Better, she thought, to give him wide berth, like a man at a party who has had too much to drink and is temporarily capable of saying anything.

But now, when she wanted an answer that nobody else knew, God's omniscience suddenly seemed useful. And from what she remembered, God also held sway in the other world that Jack belonged to.

She bowed her head and tried to remember whether or not to close her eyes. After some hesitation, she left them open.

Dear God, she began.

A shower of shreds of turquoise and white paper rained down on her upturned hands.

Clare's head snapped up.

Jack laughed.

Clare's hands flew from her lap. The scraps scattered on the carpet. An instant later, she was on her feet, her fists clenched.

"You look just like an Apache brave!" Jack crowed, his voice delighted.

His admiration seemed genuine, but Clare didn't take it as a compliment. She shook off her fighting posture and brought her heels together in a more ladylike stance.

"No one else ever jumped up to fight like that," Jack said. "Usually they're scared out of their wits."

"Do you drop paper on everyone?" Clare demanded.

"No," Jack said, with a note of pride. "They're the end-papers from a romance of the sea. It took me days to tear them up."

His voice came from overhead, as if he were inside the glass chandelier that hung from the central peak of the roof.

Clare's curiosity edged her fury aside. "Can you fly?" she asked the chandelier.

"Nope," Jack said cheerfully. The chandelier began to sway. Its crystal drops chimed and clinked. "But it doesn't hurt when I fall, so I can climb just about anything."

Clare scanned the panes of the glass ceiling that sloped

over the chandelier. There was nothing a child could have gotten purchase on to reach the fixture. "How did you get up there?" she asked.

"The joints," Jack said. "You see? The metal beams."

The copper bones of the structure, which had gone green from exposure outdoors, still retained their pink and brown sheen inside the glass house. But they were hardly ideal for climbing: just half-moon tubes, less than a hand's-breadth wide.

Jack must have caught the doubt on Clare's face. "I don't need much," he said. "It's like swimming, when you push yourself from rock to rock."

"Like flying," Clare insisted.

"No," Jack said. "Because if I don't have something to hold on to, I fall."

The chandelier gave a loud rattle, and then Jack's voice drifted down, at about the same speed a feather might drop to the ground. "But I don't . . . fall . . . very fast."

Clare lurched back, out of his trajectory.

A moment later, his voice came from a spot that would have put them face to face if Clare had been able to see him. "So there's nothing to be afraid of," he said, cheerful again.

At Clare's feet, the scattered tissue began to arrange itself in a neat pile.

Clare took a seat in one of the wine-colored wing chairs

and drew her feet up under her. The sight of the scraps of tissue, rising one by one from the carpet or sometimes blown about by short gusts from an unseen wind, was hypnotic. And it gave her a clue as to how much effort it must have taken him to tear each tiny piece.

"When other people come here," she asked, "what do you do with them?"

"It depends," he said. "I play with the books or the matches. Sometimes I laugh."

"Why?" Clare asked.

"At the things people do when they think they're alone."

"Do you talk with them?"

A scrap of turquoise hung suspended over the blue rug. It flared in the shifting sun. Then it dropped among the others.

"They pretend not to hear," Jack said, his voice subdued.

"They don't answer?" Clare asked.

"No."

"Never?"

"If it's a woman and a man, she might take his arm and ask 'What's that?'" Jack told her. "But if I talk to anyone who comes alone, they just look around. Or up at the sky."

A white flake of paper rose and dropped into the pile.

"Am I the only one to talk to you?" Clare asked.

"Tilda says goodbye," Jack told her. "Before she leaves."

"How long have you been here?"

"A while," he said.

Clare picked up a warning note: she had stumbled onto a topic he didn't want to talk about. It was rude to talk to people about death, she knew. Was it rude to talk with ghosts about it, too?

"Have you ever seen a tiger?" Jack asked.

Clare had. In Italy last year, one of her mother's friends had bought them tickets to a traveling menagerie, with a special party before the show to meet the animals, uncaged but well chained: a sleepy elephant with sequins pasted around his eyes, an ostrich whose long neck and bare legs had been daubed with red, green, and blue greasepaint, and a contemptuous tiger in a gaudy collar of paste sapphires. The elephant was bound with chain thick enough to anchor a ship. The ostrich fretted at the end of a length of red silk. But the tiger was held in place by a trio of stakes hammered into the ground at his feet, connected to his collar by taut ropes like the ones that supported the tent overhead. The configuration rendered him almost completely immobile, unless he wanted to bow his head. He never did, and he reserved another small measure of dignity: despite the stares and taunts of the curious crowd, he never glanced at them. Clare had watched the show that followed, where he snarled and pawed as he was forced to jump through a series of silver hoops and bat at a rubber ball, with a sense of outrage that had dissolved into tears as the crowd broke into their final applause.

She nodded.

"In Africa," Jack told her, "there's a lake guarded by tigers."

This wasn't true, Clare knew. Mr. Pedersen had devoted an entire lunch once to popular misconceptions concerning big cats. Zoos liked to install them together, he'd told her, but nature hadn't. Lions roamed the African savanna and parts of India. Tigers were only found in India and China and the Indochine.

"And at the bottom of the lake, there's a palace made of gold," Jack went on. "It used to stand on an island, but the water rose over it. The tigers were tamed by the palace guard, and even after the palace sank, they stayed."

"Have you been to Africa?" Clare asked.

"Not yet," Jack said. "It's the first place I'm going to go. I'll take a diving bell to loot the palace. And then I'll have enough gold to go anywhere else I want."

Despite the fact that the tigers couldn't be real, a defensive note crept into Clare's voice on behalf of the loyal beasts. "How will you get past the tigers?" Clare asked. "Are you going to shoot them?"

"Of course not," Jack said. "I'll go at night, with a torch.

Tigers are afraid of fire. And once I get on the water, they won't come after me."

Clare remembered one of the stories Mr. Pedersen had used to illustrate his luncheon lecture on big cats, about a tiger who had chewed through the wooden bars of his cage and escaped into a duchess's party, where, startled by the lights and noise, he'd dived into her bathing pool and swum the length of it, scattering terrified, half-drunk guests all along the way. This memory was followed closely by an image of a boy rowing across a dark lake by torchlight as the pale faces of half a dozen big cats cut toward him through the water from every side.

"Are you sure about that?" she asked.

"Of course," Jack said. "Have you ever tried to get a cat to take a bath?"

Clare shifted, unsure if she should encourage the dream, which he obviously treasured, or inform him of the realities, for his own good.

When she didn't answer at once, he tried another tack. "Where do you want to go?" he asked.

Clare knew what kind of answer he wanted, some kind of trade for his underwater palace: a civilization where all the people lived in treehouses and told time by bird song; a tribe of hermits who never came down from their mountaintops but visited each other by dirigible. Even if her powers of invention had failed her, she had years of experience with the wonders of the world, any of which might have suited him. But the truth rose up in her so powerfully that it swept away all possible lies.

"Home," she said.

"Home?" he repeated, incredulous. "But you could go *anywhere*," he added, as if she might not have understood the question.

Speaking the truth made Clare feel strangely light. But it also made her dizzy, as if she'd forgotten how to keep her balance without the extra weight. In any case, having spoken it at last, she refused to retreat. She raised her chin and settled back into the wing chair.

"Well, where is it?" Jack asked, as if the answer might provide some clue to her stubbornness.

"New York."

"Do you live in a mansion?"

Clare shook her head. "It's just a city house," she said. "On a little park."

"Have you heard of the Taj Mahal?" Jack demanded.

Clare nodded.

"What about the Arctic Circle?"

She nodded again.

"Don't you want to see them?" he asked.

"That's not what you said," Clare said. "You asked me

where did I want to go." She had begun to feel slightly embarrassed by the paucity of her own dreams. But at the same time, all the coasts and gangplanks she'd seen, the fountains and plazas, the circuses and cathedrals, had begun to glow with a strange new light, not because her own feelings for them had changed but because of how they might seem to Jack. It was something like the way she felt when she first saw how women eyed her mother's jewels at parties, and realized that what Clare had thought of as playthings were actually treasures to be envied.

Something struck the roof overhead. Clare glanced up. A few more raindrops rattled on the glass, then settled into a steady patter. If Clare waited for the rain to gather strength, she'd be soaked when she got to the house—which would lead to all kinds of uncomfortable questions about where she'd been.

"I have to go," she said. She crossed the room, which seemed half alive itself now with the blurred shadows of the water coursing over the glass.

Then she stepped out into the cloudburst, and ran.

TEN

AS CLARE HAD HOPED, Bridget's mother answered the door.

She had never bobbed her dark hair like some of the younger women in their set, and today it was swept back off her face in the style of an earlier decade. On her, the old style was still effective. It framed her dark eyes and set off her pale skin. Her day dress, as usual, was white, Battenberg lace over batiste. When she smiled in welcome, she focused on something just beyond Clare, as if she might be greeting a spirit who had followed her in.

"If I didn't know better," Clare's mother had observed once, "I'd say she was a laudanum eater. It's too bad she's not. At least then she could stop taking it."

"Clare," Bridget's mother said, and bent to give her an automatic kiss on the cheek. "Are you here to see Bridget?"

Clare nodded. "But I wanted to ask you something," she said. "About the other side."

For the first time, Bridget's mother met her eyes. "Anything in particular?" she asked.

Clare shrugged and held her tongue. Children, she had learned, enjoyed some of the same advantages that women did: people were prone to believe that their minds operated in some mysterious range outside the bounds of ordinary logic. Perhaps from worry that the strange logic would infect their own minds, or perhaps simply because women and children were both susceptible to tears, most people were loath to press a child for explanations, especially when a child didn't seem inclined to give one and remained quiet and polite in every other respect.

"Well," Bridget's mother said after a minute. "I was just making some lemonade. Would you like to help me with it?"

The kitchen, Clare discovered when she followed Bridget's mother, hung out over the water just like the sun porch did. Sun streamed through a wide strip of windows onto the slate floor. Beyond them, the ocean was a bright, hard blue gray, its surface troubled by thousands of small waves.

Bridget's mother took up the spot she had apparently left at the counter, a white marble shot through with black veins that faded to gray as they sank deeper in the pale stone. She sliced a lemon in half, nudged a glass juicer down the counter toward Clare, and dropped the two sides of the divided lemon beside it.

Clare picked one half up, touched its fleshy heart to the sharp tip of the juicer, and pressed down. "You've lived with ghosts before, haven't you?" she asked, as juice ran down the glass slopes into the juicer's moat.

Bridget's mother nodded and sliced another lemon into pieces. "Why do you ask?"

"Who were they?" Clare said.

"What you have to understand," Bridget's mother said in a tone that indicated she didn't really expect Clare to understand at all, "is that real ghosts have very little to do with the ghost stories you might hear from other children."

"They don't?" Clare asked, with a note of false wonder.

"Almost nothing," Bridget's mother said. "You see, they're not like you and me."

"But you've talked with them," Clare prompted.

"Ghosts very rarely speak," Bridget's mother said. "And when they're spoken to, they often retreat. That's why it's so important to work with trained mediums."

Clare had the same sensation she got when she heard people rattle off travelers' rumors about a place Clare had actually been: the realization that she already knew more than the adult who was pretending to educate her. She didn't like the feeling, but she was getting used to it. It bothered her most in moments like this, when she didn't know the answer herself, and needed one.

"Then how do you know they're there?" Clare tried.

"Most of us aren't sensitive enough to encounter them," Bridget's mother said. "I do have some sensitivity myself, but I wouldn't call it a true gift."

"What's it like?" Clare asked. "To feel a ghost?"

"Often there's a chill," Bridget's mother said. "An unseasonable chill. You have a sense that you're not alone." She added this detail as if the thought came as a relief. "And then there are apparitions."

"Ghosts that you see," Clare guessed.

Bridget's mother nodded.

"Have you seen any?" Clare asked.

Bridget's mother's hand curled around a lemon.

"There was a girl who came to our room every night in Paris," she said. "All she wore was a sleeping shift. And rubies, a thick necklace. I could see her, but Robert couldn't. He hated for me to talk about it."

"Who was she?" Clare asked.

"A nobleman's mistress," Bridget's mother said. "His wife couldn't bear a son. So when the girl delivered a boy, he took him to give to his wife as her own. The girl threw herself from our window down on the stones. He gave her the rubies in exchange for her son."

Clare had heard worse, both on palace tours and in

gossip over lunch. The story didn't shake her. But the mechanics didn't add up.

"How did you know who she was?" Clare asked. "If she didn't speak?"

"I heard the story from a servant," Bridget's mother said. "Her mother knew the girl."

"Was she the first ghost you saw?"

Bridget's mother shook her head. "That was in Italy," she said. "On my honeymoon. An old man. He sat in a chair on the balcony. The first time I saw him, I thought he was a thief. But when I screamed, he looked at me as if I'd hurt his feelings, and faded away to nothing."

"Did he come back?" Clare asked. "Like the girl?"

Bridget's mother pushed the pieces of another lemon across the marble to Clare. "Every day," she said. "I started to take breakfast with him when Robert was out."

"So you did talk with him," Clare insisted.

"He didn't speak to me," Bridget's mother said. "But he listened. Robert was convinced I had a lover. He could hear me talking, but when he came out, the old man always vanished. It made him wild." The memory of a smile flickered over her lips.

Clare thought back on Jack's chatter and pranks. He didn't seem to have much in common with these wraiths that couldn't do anything more than appear or fade away. "So why did he come, do you think?"

"The old man?"

Clare nodded.

"I'm not sure," Bridget's mother said. "Usually ghosts want to tell us something about who they were."

Clare lifted a hollow rind from the glass and pressed a fresh lemon down. For all his dreams, Jack hardly mentioned his past life. Which was strange, she realized. One of the first lessons she'd learned about people, on the endless journey that followed her father's death, was that they were almost always their own favorite subject. Over and over again, people proclaimed her both clever and charming not because they'd actually learned anything about her but because she'd spent the whole time asking questions about them. But Jack had matched her almost question for question. She hadn't recognized it at the time because there were too many other things to get used to: the voice without a face, the pages that turned themselves. But Jack's reserve would have been strange for any boy. And, if Bridget's mother could be believed, it was even out of character for a ghost.

A step creaked in the hall outside. Bridget's father appeared in the kitchen door, dressed like a movie actor in a pale silk shirt and light trousers. He took several paces before he realized anyone was there besides his wife, his face so flat and slack that Clare barely recognized him. But at the sight of Clare, a new spirit seemed to take control of him. His famous smile spread over his handsome features. He veered toward his wife, slipped his arms around her waist, and gave her a kiss on the cheek that would have been perfectly credible if Clare hadn't caught the earlier glimpse of him, before he realized she was there.

Bridget's mother tolerated the attention for a moment, then gave a light shrug, as if trying to shake off a bit of cottonwood that had settled on her shoulder.

Bridget's father turned his smile on Clare.

"Don't you look like a new day," he said. "You're growing up to be a very pretty girl. Of course, that's no surprise, since you're Cynthia's daughter."

Clare glanced at Bridget's mother, but she poured a steady stream of lemon juice onto a pyramid of sugar at the base of a clear pitcher, as if she hadn't heard a thing.

"Clare?" Bridget said. "What are you doing here?"

Clare turned toward the door, startled. She hadn't planned to go looking for Bridget until she was done pumping Bridget's mother for information. And she hadn't planned on mentioning the conversation with Bridget's mother to Bridget, whose petulance over Clare's interest in the otherworld could easily cast a shadow well into the afternoon.

Clare attempted a diversion with a fact Mack had offered her as she left the big house. "Do you want to go down to the candy store?" she asked. "They're making macarons this morning, but once they sell through, they'll close up the shop."

"I'd hardly call it a store," Bridget said. "More like a giant cigar box."

She was right. None of the storefronts that made up the town's tiny commercial district were distinguished architectural accomplishments. But the candy store in particular was a narrow, unwieldy eyesore that seemed to perch on the ridge above the beach even more precariously than its neighbors. Inside, the ceiling was inexplicably high, as if the builder had reached skyward to claim space he couldn't afford at ground level. And beyond these aesthetic objections, the shop owner, a ruddy, sharp-tongued fisherman's wife whose passion for creating French-style sweets made her deeply uneasy even as she indulged it, changed the menu every day, so that a favorite item might not appear again for a week, or even longer if a customer was unwise enough to become importunate in her pleading. The establishment didn't offer the refined experience the seasonal children were accustomed to, but it did have the clear advantage of being one of the only places in town that would tolerate young people at all. So despite Bridget's grievances, she and Clare found themselves there often.

Bridget's father fumbled in his pockets and withdrew a pair of silver dollars. He offered one first to Clare, and then to Bridget. Clare dropped her eyes as she accepted hers, half embarrassed by the generosity and half wishing she could return it to him with a stony silence that warned him to leave both her and her mother alone. But she knew that, since she was a child, even if she refused the gift, it would never be counted as anything more than her own bad manners.

"Is that enough?" Bridget's father asked, his voice uncertain. "You can get whatever you want?"

In the village candy store, where everything was sold three and four for a penny, just one of the silver dollars would buy them more sweets than either of them could eat in a week. If they spent both, they'd have enough candy to build a good-sized castle on the sand, and still be able to throw what remained into the surf by the handful. Clare pictured a flock of macarons floating out to sea: orange, lavender, and bottle green. Then they began to vanish, one by one, as fish slipped to the surface and carried them under.

Bridget dropped her silver dollar in her pocket and nodded curtly at her father, as if he were an aging servant no one could quite bear to fire.

"Well?" she said to Clare. "Aren't you coming?"

ELEVEN

GLASS JARS LINED THE walls of the shop, filled with the longest-lasting sweets: a dozen colors of rock candy crystallized on wooden wands, lemon and cinnamon drops, jawbreakers spattered with red, yellow, and blue, candy sticks in every possible flavor: apple, cherry, butterscotch, mint, sarsaparilla, lime, licorice.

The proprietor ruled her domain from behind a long counter that enclosed her pristine workspace, partially shielded by oak and glass cases that presented the day's more perishable offerings: a coconut cake, a bowl of caramels, and a few neat lines of macarons, already somewhat diminished by the day's sales.

Bridget laid her silver dollar on the counter like a gunslinger proving he was good for the next few rounds, and ordered a dozen.

"They're threepenny each," the woman warned.

Bridget didn't blink.

The woman pushed her thinning red hair out of her eyes. "You care what kind?"

"Whatever's best," Bridget said.

The woman filled a plate with an assortment of the meringues, each about the size of the silver dollar that still lay on the counter. She pushed the plate at Bridget. Bridget collected it and looked at Clare. "Don't you want anything?" she asked.

Clare, who had assumed the plate was to share, started to draw her own dollar from her pocket. But Bridget nodded impatiently at the one on the counter. "Don't be stupid," she said.

The fisherman's wife frowned at Bridget, but her frown didn't fade when she turned to Clare.

"Two, please," Clare said quickly.

"What kind?"

"Almond," Clare said, reading from the handwritten cards. "And rose."

The woman served them to her in a small white bowl. She poured water from a ceramic pitcher into two short glasses and set them on the counter as well. Then she scrawled several sums on a scrap of paper, took the silver dollar, and replaced it with a pile of smaller coins.

Bridget collected her change and pastries and headed

for the best seat in the house, a spindly table for two at the only window, which overlooked the ocean at the back of the shop.

"I think Bram is one of these men who doesn't know how much he loves a girl until he loses her," Bridget said as Clare set her dish down on the table.

Clare knew better than to offer an opinion of her own. Between the two of them, Bridget was the undisputed expert in matters of the heart. Furthermore, it wasn't territory Clare was eager to claim. She knew the boundaries of childhood. But the region of the heart was dark and uncharted, and she wasn't convinced she stood to gain by crossing into it.

"So I have a plan," Bridget said. She paused to select a macaron, then leaned forward to narrow the distance her secret would have to travel.

"I'm going to make Denby love me," she said. "Well, I think he might already," she admitted. "I'm going to make him say it."

"Denby?" Clare repeated. She'd seen the way Denby acted around Bridget: how he watched like a hawk for her reactions and brooded when her attention turned to someone else. But despite Clare's deliberate ignorance on the subject, she wasn't sure this was love. And she didn't see why wringing a confession of love from Denby should lead to one from Bram. In fact, it seemed like a step that could only complicate the situation.

"Of course, we couldn't be together," Bridget went on. "Since I'll never love him. But then Bram will have to do something, because he'll see what it would mean to lose me." She selected another macaron, popped it into her mouth, and leaned back.

It was clear to Clare that Bridget expected more than a nod in response. But Clare also knew that questioning the plan would only result in recrimination. So she settled on a tactic that was almost always safe: asking Bridget to expand on her vision.

"What will you do then?" Clare asked.

Bridget nodded as if this were a sensible question, and one which she'd already given some thought to.

"Well, we'll be married," she said. "They'll say we're too young, but I know I love him. And if they resist, we'll run away."

This, Clare knew, was impossible. Bridget might be the expert in love, but Clare knew the rules of the world. "Where will you get money?" she asked.

Bridget pulled a handful of coins from her pocket and let them scatter over the table. "There's money everywhere you look," she said.

"Where will you live?"

"We don't have to worry about that yet," Bridget said. "We just need to go away together. Then they'll have to let us be married."

Deep inside Clare, a warning bell rang. She'd seen her mother kiss a handful of men, but there was something else her mother refused them, something that had to do with nights spent in hotel rooms. The details weren't clear to Clare. But she could see they weren't clear to Bridget, either. And from the glimpses of greed, anger, and agony Clare had seen when men argued about it with her mother, Clare knew it couldn't be the simple prank Bridget seemed to think it was.

"But don't you want a wedding?" Clare asked, in an attempt to protect her friend through an appeal to a competing desire. She garnished the dream with a pair of Bridget's particular weaknesses. "With French lace? And peonies?"

A shadow crossed Bridget's face, but it only took her a moment to fold Clare's offering into her own larger fantasy. "Of course," she said. "When we come back, we'll have all that."

Clare crossed her arms over her belly.

Bridget frowned. "I thought you'd be happy for me," she said.

"I am," Clare insisted. "It's just—"

"You don't understand how things have been," Bridget interrupted. The desperation in her voice was the first true note in her performance all morning. "It's impossible to live with them."

Clare reached across the table and laid her hand on Bridget's.

Bridget tolerated the gesture for only a moment before she shook it off.

"There's no need for dramatics," she said. "It's not like I'm one of those orphans from the war."

Clare's fingers closed around her almond macaron.

Bridget regarded Clare, her expression now magnanimous.

"Who are you going to marry?" she asked.

On guard, Clare shrugged.

"Well, who are you in love with?" Bridget asked patiently.

Clare shook her head.

Bridget raised her eyebrows and pursed her lips. "That may be for the best," she said. "Love matches don't always end in happiness. Of course, if you love someone like I love Bram, you have no choice." She glanced out to sea. "What about Denby?" she suggested.

"Denby?" Clare repeated.

Bridget nodded. "After Bram and I go away," she said.

"He'll be brokenhearted, but you can tend to him in his hour of need."

"I don't love Denby," Clare tried. But her appeal to the strange logic of the heart was amateur, and came too late. Her refusal to deal with it before had left her exposed.

"But you don't love anybody," Bridget insisted. "And what's wrong with poor Denby?"

The sheer number of answers Clare could give to this question made her feel defensive for Denby, the way she did when other children mocked him for his air of command and his bad temper when challenged. They saw him as ridiculous because they'd never benefited from his leadership: never enjoyed stolen cake on a roped-off balcony, never discovered a new cave instead of dawdling on the beach. She wouldn't have let someone else list his faults in front of her, and she rebelled at the thought of reeling them off herself.

Instead, she shrugged again.

"Then that's settled," Bridget said, with a brisk nod.

The ease with which Bridget had dispensed with Clare's whole future nettled Clare. She might not be an expert on love, but she wasn't willing to be disposed of so neatly.

"What about Teddy?" she asked.

"What about him?" Bridget demanded, her expression suddenly fierce.

Clare had meant to put up resistance, but she didn't

want to start a war. She retreated into innocence. "Who do you think he'll marry?" she asked.

Bridget's features softened to their customary worldliness. "Well, that hardly matters, does it?" she said. "He'll always do what he wants.

"It's not the same for us," she went on, in the low, urgent voice usually reserved for telling weird stories at night. "Once a girl gives her heart away, we can never love again."

Twelve

HAT AFTERNOON, WHEN CLARE returned to the glass house, half a dozen pale pink tulips lay on the mossy flagstone.

They had been yanked out near the root, not neatly clipped. Their broken stems were white and fleshy. A few of the petals bore the telltale creases of careless handling. Clare glanced at the nearest garden, just beyond the glade. A whole corner of it had been denuded, giving the planting a lopsided effect, like a preening bird with a missing tail feather.

Clare knelt over the flowers on the stone.

"Do you like them?" Jack asked.

His voice came from a few steps away, but a current ran over her skin when she heard it, like the strands of blue electricity that raced silently over the face of a glass globe she'd seen at an exhibition in Paris the previous summer. The globe had been fashioned with relief maps of the continents and oceans. The adults around her saw it as whimsy, but

Clare's mind had filled with the havoc that kind of lightning would wreak on the tiny world: mountains split, steeples smoking, ships splintered. The thought of a similar current playing over her own skin made her uneasy. But the flowers fading on the stone filled her with tenderness. Without water, they'd be nothing but dry grass in a few hours.

This, unlike the other feeling, she could do something about. She collected the pulpy stems into the crook of her arm, careful not to crush the blossoms.

"Do you?" Jack asked again, but his voice rose with satisfaction.

Clare stood with the tulips and scanned the yard. Along the fieldstone foundation that supported the white brick of the house, she saw the glint of a faucet and below it, black loops of rubber hose.

She started up the hill.

"Wait!" Jack exclaimed, startled. "Where are you going?"

"They need water," Clare said.

Jack kept pace alongside her. "But you just got here," he protested.

"Well, come with me," Clare said, somewhat impatiently. She crested the hill and darted across the upper lawn to the lip of the garden. There, she felt a faint remorse over her sharp tone.

"They're so pretty," she explained. "They just shouldn't go without water for long."

Jack didn't answer. She glanced around, half expecting to catch sight of some new prank: yards of ribbon streaming from the branches of the oak tree, a stand of daisies dancing under his invisible hand.

"Jack?" she asked.

Still nothing.

She glanced up at the windows of the house. Each of them reflected its own shard of the yard. Anybody might be inside, looking out. She didn't have time to play whatever game Jack was up to now.

She darted around the corner to the wide door of Mack's workshop. It stood ajar. Clare slipped in.

A few glass jars glinted temptingly on the shelves above Mack's cluttered workbench, but they were filled with nails or sand or seeds, and Clare knew she couldn't empty one of them without him noticing. But on the floor by the door was a promising jumble of buckets. One of those, she guessed, would be hard to miss.

When she turned the faucet on, the black hose twitched as if it had come alive. Warm water coughed out of the spout. One-handed, still cradling the tulips in her other arm, Clare twisted the end of the hose into the bucket she'd commandeered. Water rose against the silver walls. When it neared the top, she twisted the faucet off. Then she hurried down the hill.

Annoyed by whatever prank he'd just tried to play, Clare stalked into the glass house in silence. If Jack wanted to disappear like that, he could think what to say next.

And the torn white ends of the tulip stems still needed to be cut if the blooms were going to last. She set the pail down on a rug and began to investigate the buffet.

The first drawer she pulled open revealed a collection of mismatched tapers wrapped in crushed tissue. As she pushed the paper aside, the drawer above it stuttered open of its own accord. She started, then slapped it back into place.

It stuttered open again. "What are you looking for?" Jack asked.

"A knife," Clare said.

The haunted drawer rattled shut. "What for?" A hint of excitement had crept into Jack's voice, as if he welcomed the possibility of stripping branches or fending off bandits, or anything else a boy might do with a knife.

"The flowers," Clare told him. "I need to cut the stems."

"We don't have an actual knife," Jack admitted. "But there's a letter opener under the buffet."

The buffet was made of dark mahogany with a low arch,

only about two inches high, between its solid feet. Clare got to her knees, but hesitated to reach in to the darkness. "What's it doing there?"

"I wanted it for a sword, but it was too heavy to hold," Jack said. "And then I couldn't lift it after it fell."

Something skittered in the shadows. Clare jerked back.

"It's okay," Jack said. Another skitter, and the small face of a bird emerged from under the buffet. The bird's head was made from translucent white stone, with a tiny red gem for an eye. "There," Jack said.

Clare picked up the letter opener. The bird's head curved into wings, gilded with gold and crusted with other tiny gems: blue, black, and green. Its figure formed the handle of a dull brass blade.

"Will it work?" Jack asked.

"Let's see," Clare said. She took a metal serving tray from the clutter on the buffet, pulled a stem from the bucket, laid it on the tray, and neatly sliced off the bruised end of the stalk. Instantly, she replaced it in the water.

"That works!" Jack crowed beside her. The discarded end of the stalk began to roll merrily on the metal tray in celebration.

Clare pulled another stem from the water. A few minutes later all the tulips were neatly trimmed, and Clare had disposed of the broken ends in the myrtle outside the door.

She settled down on the rug near the divan, beside the bucket of tulips, which she'd placed on the low table. Her anxiety for their survival quelled, she could finally take in how beautiful the blossoms were. No self-respecting florist would ever have delivered such a meager bouquet. But because there were so few blooms, each one seemed to have a life of its own: this one was pale enough to faint; that one's petal had been forked by a blow.

"They were so heavy," Jack said. "Do you like them?"

"Yes," she answered. The softness of her own voice startled her. It was the voice she might have used to answer her father when he tucked her in at night. She hadn't sounded like that since she was a little girl.

The realization she had dropped her guard turned her mind suspicious.

"Where did you go?" she asked. "When I went up to the house?"

"I was with you," Jack said. But his voice turned up at the end, like a question.

Clare hated to be told something she knew wasn't true. Adults did it to children all the time. But when children did it to each other, it had a special flavor of betrayal. If children didn't tell each other the truth, how would any of them ever understand the world? With Jack, it was even worse. She couldn't see his hands to tell if he was rich or poor, his clothes to guess if he came from Boston or New York, his face to see if he was interested or bored. She couldn't know anything about him except what he told her. The thought that he could be making everything up, like an older kid telling a little one that chewing gum grew on trees, made her feel foolish, and furious.

"Where did I get the bucket?" she demanded.

"Mack's bench," Jack tried: another question.

Clare gave her head a single hard shake. "It was by the door," she said, and drew her feet under her to get up.

"Wait," Jack said.

Clare waited, her eyebrows raised. Now he was the one who sounded like a confused kid.

"I tried to come with you," Jack said. "I couldn't."

The defeat in his voice gave Clare the uncomfortable feeling that somehow she was the bully, not him.

"Why not?" she asked.

The silence lasted so long that Clare glanced around the glass house, wondering if he'd disappeared again.

But when he spoke, his voice came from exactly where it had been, on the floor beside her. "I can see the big house from here," he said quietly. "But when I try to get close, there's only mist."

"Mist?" Clare said.

"Like fog, before the sun burns it off," Jack said. "Did you ever stand inside a bank while it rolls out to sea?"

Clare shook her head, no.

"It's so bright, it hurts your eyes," Jack said. "But you can't see anything."

Clare looked up to the house on the hill. Vines obscured the view and dust clouded the panes. But there was no sign of mist anywhere in the yard.

"I tried to go with you," Jack went on. "But you disappeared, and I got lost in the mist."

"It's all around the big house?" Clare asked. Her imagination blanketed the red peaks and white brick in thick clouds.

"No," Jack said. "It's all around this one."

The phantom fog in her mind rolled down the hill and curled around the glass house, blotting out the lawn, the oaks, the occasional gardens, the lilacs, and the forest beyond. Clare pulled her knees up. "Right up to the glass?" she asked, her voice low, as if to keep the fog from overhearing.

"You see the redbud tree?" Jack asked.

Clare nodded. The delicate trunk divided into slim, trailing branches near the foot of the hill, maybe twenty paces from the glass house.

"It starts there," he said. "And just past the oak tree. And a ways into the forest."

The landmarks he chose described a large, clumsy circle, perhaps fifty paces in diameter, around the glass house.

"It's like a ring," Clare said.

"That's right," Jack said, with a teacher's pleasure at a quick student.

"But you don't see it all the time."

"Only if I go over there," Jack said. "I don't like to."

"It's always by the redbud tree?" Clare asked. "It never moves?"

"No," Jack said. "It doesn't."

When Jack spoke next, his voice came from halfway across the glass house, drifting toward the door.

"But I can climb all the trees, as high as I want," he said. "There's no mist up there."

Clare scrambled to her feet. By the time she followed him out into the glade, the vines that covered the sides of the house had already started to sag and twitch under Jack's invisible weight. When he reached the top of the house, which crested just below the lowest branches of the young maples that surrounded it, glass rattled faintly and the topmost vines shivered. Then a single rose seemed to leap from the roof of the glass house into the branches of the maple tree.

The maple branches swayed, and sprang back into place. For a long moment, Clare lost track of Jack. Then, from the topmost branches of the tree, the tiny petals of the unlucky rose began to rain down into the glade.

THIRTEEN

"CAREFUL," DENBY SAID SHARPLY. "If you get yourself killed, they'll never let the rest of us come back."

Bridget wobbled on an outcrop of black rock with considerable flair, caught his hand, and swooned against him. Denby's body stiffened at the contact, as if steeling himself against a blow. But when he glanced at her, his eyes were bright with something like hunger.

"I'm sorry," Bridget said, her voice full of promise, not remorse. She righted herself, shook her shoulders, and began to pick her way nimbly down the cliff.

Denby watched her go.

He and Bram had arrived at Bridget and Teddy's early that afternoon and insisted that Bridget, Teddy, and Clare follow them to the beach. Teddy had demanded an explanation as to why he should leave the wicker couch he was sprawled on, but Denby had flatly refused, which created a mystery far more potent than any promises Denby could have made.

So they had all walked up the white shell road to Denby's rented house, where the set of half-ruined stone steps led down the cliff to the beach, just a few yards from the mouth of the cave.

By day, sun lit the water in the cave a rich turquoise and reflected up on the rough walls in pale strands that shifted and rocked with each pulse of the tide. Bram darted in first. Shoes in hand, Denby and Bridget clambered easily over the rocks. But now that Clare could see everything, she could hardly believe she'd ever gotten to the other side.

The rocks were the size of suitcases or traveling trunks, their spines sharp, their faces slick. Water hissed and fizzed between them. Everyone else leapt from stone to stone. But Clare stood with both bare feet on a single rock, surveyed for another likely spot, then took up a firm position before choosing the next.

"Hurry up," Bridget called. "Someone's going to see you."

"You're holding up the whole caravan," Teddy echoed from a few rocks behind Clare.

Rattled, Clare stepped blindly from one rock to the

next, where the sharp edge she landed on opened a long, shallow cut from the ball of her foot to the arch. She jerked back from the sting of salt, and turned the sole up to find a thin line of bright red. Where the blood met water on her skin, it blossomed and faded to rose.

"I cut my foot," Clare called back.

"So did I," Denby retorted. "It's salt water. They use it to clean wounds."

"You learn that in the war?" Teddy asked.

The sting of the wound pushed Clare on toward the ledge. But it also made her clumsy. A few rocks before she reached the cave, her foot turned. She tried to right herself with another step, but only reeled. The sea and the sharp rocks swung sickeningly around her, and her mind filled with fear of the phantom pain of a fall on her shin, her knees, her side.

A steady arm caught her around the waist. "You all right?" Bram asked.

Clare listed against him, then straightened, surprised by the heat that seeped from his arm through her thin dress.

She nodded.

"Here," Bram said, and pointed to the wide, flat plane of a nearby rock.

Clare stepped where he pointed. He stepped along with

her and found his footing on a narrower spot, his arm still around her waist.

"Here," he said again, and pointed to another rock. When they reached that one: "There."

A few steps later, they'd gained the ledge.

"That's one way to get a girl to hold your hand," Teddy observed.

Instantly, Bram released her. Bridget gave Clare a hard look. Up ahead, Denby's voice rang out. "Come on," he said. "We're almost there."

"Thank you," Clare told Bram.

Bridget and Teddy disappeared after Denby, but Bram waited as Clare dropped her shoes on the stone. She made an attempt to wipe the blood from her sole, but it only smeared. After a minute, she gave up and slipped the shoes on.

"Go ahead," Bram said, nodding into the dark.

Clare's foot was ginger from the cut, but she stiffened her back against the pain. Around them, the sun flashed and twisted on the curved walls.

This time, she didn't falter when the passage narrowed and grew dim. But when the blind turns let them out into the hidden cavern, she stopped short.

An entire suite of furniture had appeared on the waxy white rock in the center of the room: a baby-blue couch with flourishes of cherry wood, a leather armchair with tufts of horsehair spilling from a cut in one flank, a red loveseat with a high arched back, a green velvet ottoman with long gold fringe that fell all the way from the seat to the stone two feet below. There was even a low table in the center, bearing an assortment of mismatched oil lamps whose unsteady light turned strange among the fingers of rock in the high corners of the cave.

Bridget had already taken up a corner of the red loveseat, pulled her feet up, leaned back into the curve, and arranged her skirt in a half-moon sweep. She glanced away pointedly when Clare appeared.

Teddy, beside the loveseat, shook his head and laughed. "I'll be damned," he said.

"What do you think?" Bram asked, beside Clare.

The eagerness in his eyes made it hard for Clare to hold his gaze.

"How did you get this all down here?" she asked.

"You threw it all down the hill?" Teddy said.

"Where did it come from?" Bridget broke in.

"Our places," Denby said, with an unconvincing attempt at nonchalance.

"No one noticed?" Clare asked as she and Bram came up.

"We carried it down," Bram explained. "Except for the blue couch. Denby made a pulley for that."

"A pulley?" Bridget repeated.

Denby nodded. "A simple one. I lashed it with rope and we let it out around one of the boulders."

"I carried the red one down by myself," Bram told Clare.

"It's so *comfortable*," Bridget said, and gave a little wriggle.

Clare sat in the corner of the blue couch. Bram took a seat on it too, splitting the difference: not beside her, but not on the other side, either. Teddy settled into the damaged armchair.

Up close, it was clear that all the furniture had also suffered in its travels. One side of the ottoman's gold fringe was shrunken and stiff, probably from a dip in salt water. A water stain spread over the blue cushion between Clare and Bram, and the velvet was smeared with tar and dusted by sand. The low table had sustained several gouges that cut through its deep varnish to the raw wood below. Only Bram's loveseat seemed to have survived more or less intact.

"What will we do about this?" Clare asked, wiping at a smear of tar. "Before we put it back?"

Denby was the only one still standing. "We're not putting it back," he said.

"We're not?" Bram said, surprised.

"They don't know it's gone now," Denby said. "No one will realize until after we've left—if they even do then. And who would think of looking here?"

Bram frowned. Clare's heart tugged at the lonely fate of the furniture Denby had just consigned forever to the dark cave.

Denby took his seat on the green and gold ottoman like a king giving the signal that court was now open.

Bridget sat up. "What should we do now?" she asked.

Denby's glance at her carried clear contempt at the suggestion that the small miracle he'd already accomplished demanded any embellishment.

Bridget was undeterred. "We could play post office," she said.

Clare had never played post office, but Bridget had learned it last summer in Nice. The game didn't have any clear rules, or a winner or loser. One player, the postman, had to leave the group. When the postman returned, the rest of the party announced who among them had to go out to receive their "letter"—a kiss.

"Post office is for kids," Teddy said.

"No, it isn't," said Bridget.

"It's for kids who can't get anyone to kiss them," Teddy amended.

"That's not true," Bridget said.

"Sure it is," Teddy said. "How many people have you kissed?"

"Plenty," Bridget answered. But then her face flickered, uncertain. Clare knew Bridget wasn't lying. She was wondering if she should have told the truth.

"When you weren't playing post office?" Teddy pressed.

"That's none of your business," Bridget said.

Clare didn't know what adventure Denby had had in mind when he dragged the furniture down the cliff, but this clearly wasn't it. He looked from Bridget to Teddy with unconcealed fury. "I don't think any of us really care how many boys Bridget has kissed," he said.

The triumph that flared in Bridget's eyes at this was replaced almost instantly by a wounded look.

Teddy raised his hands in mock surrender. "All right, all right," he said.

It only took a moment for his gaze to wander from Bridget to Clare. "What about you, Clare?" Teddy asked. "How many people have you kissed?"

Beside her on the couch, Clare could feel Bram shift.

She stared at Teddy, her gaze steady, with the unblinking silence that sometimes worked with adults: made them forget unpleasant questions, or replace old questions with new ones.

Teddy just laughed. "You haven't kissed anyone," he said. "Have you?"

Heat rushed to Clare's cheeks, but she quickly calculated that it was probably too dark for the others to see. Teddy was right. Until now, she'd never cared if she ever kissed anyone. But neither had anyone else.

"She didn't say that," Bridget snapped.

Teddy didn't even glance at his sister. "Tell me I'm wrong, Clare," he said, his gaze still fixed on Clare. "Tell us all the boys you've kissed."

Even Denby watched Clare now with something approaching interest.

"Come on," Teddy said. "Tell us what you've done with them." He leaned forward, his legs spread wide, his elbows on his knees.

Suddenly, Bram was on his feet. "Leave her alone," he said.

Bridget looked up at Bram, stricken.

Teddy eased back in his chair, his eyebrows high, his grin twisted.

"Sit down," Denby ordered.

Bram watched Teddy for a long moment. Then he sat back down again.

Bridget's gaze shifted to Clare, where it hardened.

FOURTEEN

CLARE'S MOTHER UNHOOKED THE thread of tiny freshwater pearls from the back of her neck and hung it on one of the red lilies Tilda had brought up to her that morning. The strand hung down over her dressing table like a piece of loose rigging.

Clare shifted from one foot to the other in the doorway.

Her mother turned back with a smile. "Hello, love," she said.

Clare took up a perch at the foot of her mother's bed.

"Adeline Lewis is hosting a bridge party on the beach," her mother told her. "I doubt she was expecting children, but I also doubt the conversation will rise beyond a child's comprehension. Would you like to come along?"

Clare shook her head. "I just came home," she said.

"Did you have a good time with Bridget?" her mother asked.

Clare hesitated.

Her mother rummaged through the velvet chambers of her jewelry case and pulled another necklace out. This one was an old-fashioned setting, blue topaz petals and emerald leaves on a white gold vine.

Clare knew immediately where it must have come from. Her mother's girlhood bangles were all paste, carved wood, hand-painted glass over butterfly wings. And the vine was too ornate to date from the past few years, when all the jewelry was made to look like airplanes or skyscrapers.

Her mother lifted her chin to show off the gems. "What do you think?" she asked.

Her mother's reflection was strange in the glass: her eyes familiar, but traded, the wrong side of her smile crooked, the wrong eyebrow arched.

It might have been this strangeness that gave Clare the courage to ask, "Did Daddy give you that?"

Her mother's hands froze above her head, like a dancer listening for the strains of the next movement. Then she turned around. Her eyes hadn't filled with tears, as Clare had feared. In fact, they seemed to have a kind of question in them. "He did," she said.

"When?" Clare asked.

Her mother touched the jewels at her throat.

"The day we got married," she said. To Clare's surprise,

her mother's lips twisted as if she'd just heard a joke. "He told me he'd had it for weeks, but he waited until the deal was sealed so I couldn't raise enough money to run off before the wedding."

Her smile broke into a grin at the memory.

Then she stood and gathered Clare into the sheer layers of fabric at her waist. Clare's hands found hiding spots in her mother's skirts. Her mother smoothed Clare's hair.

"He loved you so much," her mother said.

This was a benediction her mother had said over Clare a hundred times since her father's death. It might even have been what Clare had come in search of. But for the first time since his death, the familiar words didn't settle her heart.

Her own memories of her father had long since worn thin, like faces in a photograph that faded a bit more each time she touched her finger down to point at them. And they had only ever been a child's memories. She had never been old enough to study him the way she now studied everyone she met. Even when her memories had been whole, they had never been enough to tell her what kind of man he'd been.

But the more Clare learned about other men and boys, the more she wished she knew about him. And despite the story her mother had just told her, Clare knew she couldn't learn what she wanted to know by asking. She needed to know things you could only learn if you watched and listened. But she would never see him again.

She breathed in the scent of talc and perfume from her mother's dress. Her mother kissed the top of Clare's head and pulled free.

"Are you sure you don't want to come to Adeline's?" she asked. "She's promising chilled grapefruit with bowls of sugar to dip it in. Apparently Walter's workmen just uprooted an entire orchard to make way for another one of his Florida hotels. He had them send up a dozen crates, and now it's up to us to dispose of them."

Clare shook her head.

"Once again, you're absolutely right," her mother said. "I wouldn't go either if I still had the privileges of a child." She gathered up a chiffon wrap, kissed Clare again, and went out. Her skirts whispered down the stairs with a shush like the end of a lullaby.

Clare found Tilda in the kitchen, surrounded by a queen's ransom of silver. The counter overlooking the circle drive was crowded with flatware, stacks of serving trays, pitchers, carving knives and ladles, the scrambled elements of several tea services, and a small army of bud vases massed at the foot of a gravy boat shaped like a goose. Most of these were arrayed to the right of the sink, their features shadowed by tarnish, but a small contingent stood to the left at high shine.

With white paste from a small mixing bowl, Tilda cut a gleaming path down the center of a broad oval platter. This one hadn't turned a uniform black: the delicate scrollwork was clouded with purple and copper, almost like the stains flame made on the stones of a hearth. In fact, all the tarnished silver looked as if it were coated in soot. It was hard to believe that all it had passed through was time, not some great blaze.

Clare padded over to the table by the window and sat down. At the scrape of the chair on tile, Tilda turned around.

By now, anywhere else, Clare would have heard the history of the house so many times she'd already be tired of it. Servants loved to talk about the families they served, and their stories were even better than serials in magazines, because each servant knew a different piece. This one had seen the young master bury something in the garden. This one had discovered the old mistress dressed up in a parade uniform from the last war. And then they could argue for hours about whether he'd been burying a gun or a book, or if the uniform belonged to her father or lover—and how all this fit with the other family secrets they'd collected over the years along with the soiled laundry and dirty plates.

But Tilda remained her own locked room. Other maids liked to teach Clare a thing or two about the world, or confess their secrets to her. If Clare hung around long enough, they might even forget she was there. Not Tilda. She regarded Clare with a suspicion so deep it came as a kind of compliment. Clare's useful poses never worked on her. But that was because, unlike all the other maids, Tilda seemed to realize that Clare had a mind of her own.

"The roses look nice," Clare tried: an indirect approach to the topic of the glass house.

Tilda's eyes narrowed for battle. At first Clare thought she'd made a tactical error to even touch on the subject. But Tilda was remembering a much older fight.

"She said roses would never climb that high," she said, as if in retort to someone only she could see.

Clare struggled to keep the elation from her face. She hadn't imagined she could lure Tilda so quickly into the past. But now that she was there, the trick was not to break the flow of her thoughts. "She should see it now," Clare ventured.

"They wouldn't even pay for the first plants," Tilda said, her outrage at the old slight still fresh. "He had to bring cuttings from his mother's garden." She wiped a shining band across the belly of the platter in her hands. "You know what she told him? When they first came here from the city?"

Clare shook her head, but Tilda was past the need for encouragement.

"She only wanted a *lawn*," Tilda said, with the glee of one believer repeating blasphemy to another. "She was tired of all the fuss about gardens." Tilda paused to let the absurdity of this sink in as she rinsed the platter and set it aside. Then she picked up a squat teapot and stripped the tarnish from its handle with one sure stroke.

"So Mack would come in with a box of myrtle, or Star of Bethlehem. And he'd ask her, isn't this pretty? He had to beg permission for every flower in that garden, one by one. She laughed at his rose cuttings. She only agreed to let him put them in because she didn't think they'd survive the summer."

Clare looked out at the garden, which now spread a good ten feet from the foundation, each plant a flag of victory. Her gaze traveled down to the glass house, now completely overgrown by Mack's climbing roses.

"How long did it take them to get so high?" she asked.

Tilda rinsed the teapot and picked up a towel to wipe it dry.

"He forced a blossom the second year," she said with pride. "He sent it up to her the day the boy was born."

A chill ran over Clare's skin. This was the first time anyone had admitted that another child had ever lived in the house, despite all the evidence of the room upstairs. But Clare also knew Tilda hadn't trusted her with a confidence. She'd made a slip. Any moment now, she might come to her senses and retreat into stony silence. But if Clare could startle her with an unexpected fact, Tilda might give something else away.

"Jack?" Clare asked. "Jack Cunningham?"

It was a wild gamble, because to speak Jack's name threw all Clare's own cards on the table. But when Tilda turned around, there was no shock or sorrow on her face. Instead, she seemed bemused, with a faint new respect for Clare.

"Where on earth did you hear of Jack Cunningham?" Tilda asked.

Clare had thought Jack's name would rattle Tilda. But in her rush not to lose the moment, she hadn't considered the next obvious step: that she'd be asked how she learned it. She pressed back against the unforgiving curve of the wooden chair. "Around," she said.

"And what do you hear about him?" Tilda said, her eyes now bright with amusement.

Clare shrugged.

"Well," Tilda said. "You can meet him right now if you like. He just went by outside with Mack."

Clare stared at her in shock.

"Well," Tilda said, and nodded at the door to Mack's shop. "Go on." It was a command, not a suggestion.

Clare rose, unsteady. When she reached the door, she glanced back. Tilda's face was set, her eyebrows raised, her chin jutting like the prow of a ship. Clare stepped through the door and pulled it shut behind her.

She waited for a few breaths at the top of the half flight of stairs that led down to Mack's workshop. The unfinished walls were hung with a whole museum of curiosities: garden tools with handles rubbed smooth as driftwood, a pail full of the stubs of beeswax tapers, a few of Mack's work shirts, soft with age, and a neat collection of herbs tied with scraps of ribbon and labeled. A sturdy shelf built into the slope of the stairs held jars of peaches, tomatoes, pickles, and wax beans. As Clare's eyes adjusted, she realized the shadows beyond the jars were full of roses, dozens of them, dried and stacked bloom to bloom like the skulls Clare's mother had taken her to see, packed cheek to cheek in the Paris catacombs.

Tilda's tread on the other side of the door startled Clare into motion again. She clattered down the steps to the workshop. On the far side, the door to the yard stood slightly ajar. A thick band of sunshine fell through it, but she had no intention of going out there before she'd had a chance to collect her thoughts.

The forest, she calculated, began only a few yards from the shed door. She could listen to make sure the coast was clear, then dart out into the brambles, just beyond. From there, if she circled the yard through the woods, she might be able to catch sight of Mack and find out what Tilda had been talking about.

Clare crept to the door to listen. Besides a few birds trading scraps of song, the yard was quiet. She pushed the door wide and dashed out just as a pair of men came around the corner from the circle drive.

The first was Mack, in a faded plaid shirt, carrying a bucket full of onions and blue flowers. The other man was a bit younger, his hair darker than Mack's, his face browned where Mack's was red, his glance curious, while Mack's was guarded. He stood almost a whole head taller than Mack, but like Mack he was dressed in dungarees, the sleeves of his blue shirt rolled up.

All three of them stopped short.

Clare composed her face in what she hoped were lines of innocence. Mack gave her his ready smile, but with a trace of consternation at discovering her in the door of his workshop. The other man looked at her with mild curiosity.

Clare collected herself first, with the swift realization that if she dove in now, she could head off any awkward questions. "I'm Clare," she said, and held her hand out to the other man.

He shook it.

"Jack," he said.

The pang that sounded in Clare's chest echoed out through her shoulders and the back of her head. She was used to masking these pangs. She'd had to learn, in the months after her father's death, when well-meaning strangers asked her about him again and again. She couldn't weep every time she was forced to explain that he was gone, so she'd learned to wall off her heart and steady her face so it didn't give anything away. Still, the effort always left her slightly deaf.

"Clare's staying with us for the summer," Mack explained to the other Jack. "Jack has the farm just down the road," he told Clare. "He came over to bring us a few things."

"Well, I remember how Tilda loves delphiniums," the other Jack said. "And that you could never make them grow for love or money after I left."

"I'm not sure I'd put it that way," Mack said.

"Then you've got some this year?" the other Jack said. "Let's see them."

"Not every garden needs delphiniums," Mack retorted.

Clare studied the other Jack's face, listening for any echo of the Jack she knew. Aside from the slight coastal lilt in both their voices, she didn't hear one. Did turning into a man completely erase a boy? And if the man stood here in front of her, what was the boy doing in the glass house?

"Jack *Cunningham?*" Clare asked.

The question was uncalculated, a graceless attempt to cut through her own confusion. But it had an immediate effect.

The other Jack glanced at her in surprise.

Mack's eyebrows drew together. "Clare," he said, still with a servant's deference but a note of warning in his voice. "How do you happen to know Mr. Cunningham?"

"Tilda told me you were in the yard," Clare said. Before either of them could realize that this didn't really answer the question, she pressed on with one of her own.

"You used to work here?" she asked.

The other Jack nodded. "When I was a boy," he said.

"Did you help Mack plant the roses down by the glass house?"

The other Jack laughed. "Afraid not," he said, looking at Mack. "You had those in years before I came on the place."

Mack nodded.

"You see, Mack here is *much older* than me," the other Jack said, in a tone clearly meant not to teach her, but to tease Mack. "He was a grown man when I was only fifteen."

Mack stifled a grin and took a friendly swipe at him.

The other Jack eluded him with a step. "But I can't take any credit for the gardens," the other Jack went on. "Unless you find a delphinium Mack hasn't managed to kill. I was only here one summer, until—" A glance passed between the two men. Clare wouldn't have recognized it if she hadn't seen it so often after her father's death: a silent agreement between men not to talk about something that had hurt them. "Until summer's end," the other Jack finished.

The ground under her feet seemed to roll gently, like the deck of a ship. Clare kept her balance, with effort. "Well," she said. "I was just going out to take a walk."

"Careful on the east side of the house," Mack called as she started down the hill. "All my tools are still lying out."

Clare nodded to show she'd heard. Then, without making any attempt at concealment, she cut across the lawn into the grove of young maples that shaded the glass house. When she reached it she looked back. Both of the men were gone.

On the mossy flagstone, she stared so hard through the door of the glass house that the vines and reflections blurred with the furniture in the room, and all of them began to reel. As she glared, the glass rattled: a sound that might have been a finger tap, or might have been the wind.

Then she turned on her heel and strode back up the hill.

FIFTEEN

NO ONE ELSE HAD arrived yet at the switchback steps that led down to the beach.

Clare checked up the cliff, toward Bram's and Denby's houses, and down the coast, toward Bridget and Teddy's, but the shell road that ran along the bluff was deserted. No one else had arrived yet at the switchback steps that led down to the beach. So she started down the shifting sand of the hairpin path alone, with lurches and long slides she would never have allowed herself if anyone else were there to see. On the last turn, the sand gave way beneath her heels and carried her in a sifting flume several yards toward the shoreline.

"Hey!" someone said behind her, his voice loud with alarm. "Careful!"

Clare turned, still unsteady from the descent.

Bram sat in the narrow strip of shade at the foot of the cliff, on a small rug. He had risen up on his haunches, probably as she skidded onto the sand, but when she turned, he eased back. "You all right?" he said.

Clare nodded. The giddiness of the fall had faded, but the discovery that she was not alone left her off-balance. Despite the obvious explanations, Bram's sudden appearance, with the rug on the sand, had all the force of magic.

Bram patted the carpet beside him, where there was just room for one more person. "Come sit," he said.

Clare climbed the slight rise into the shade and sat beside him. The rug was so small that their bare arms brushed.

"Denby wanted a rug," Bram told her. "They've got half a dozen of them rolled up in the back room of his place, but he says the rugs in my house are actual Persian. He wanted me to take the one from the sunroom, but they'd miss it the second I did. I got this from the bar downstairs," he said, patting the low nap. "He's just going to have to live with it." But the defensive note in his voice betrayed him. He was already steeling himself against Denby's wrath.

Clare craned her neck to see up the hill. "Where's everyone else?"

Bram shrugged. "Maybe they got stuck at a séance."

Clare felt herself flush, as if he'd just walked past a place where she had hidden something. She took a sideways glance at him, hoping to find he had been looking out to sea and missed it. But he watched her steadily.

"Have you ever been to one?" she asked in confusion, then frowned at herself. This would have been polite conversation at the captain's table, but somehow it didn't seem to fit here with Bram.

"A séance?" he said.

Clare nodded.

Bram scooped up dry sand with a nearby shell and let it pour in a veil over the shell's serrated edge. He gave an almost imperceptible nod.

"You have?" Clare said, surprised.

"My dad," Bram said. "He wanted to talk with my mother."

This struck Clare as a serious error in judgment. The spirits of Bridget's mother's séances, she knew, were only a new variety of entertainment: more animated than dolls, more absorbing than a carnival, but weaker and less menacing than actual people. But Clare's longing for her father cut so deep that she required a heaven to hide him, and a God to keep that heaven. The difference between the sham magic of a séance and the dark grave she'd seen her father's casket lowered into was so profound that they had never seemed to have anything to do with one another. But now an almost ungovernable hope stirred in the roots of her heart.

"What did she say?" she asked.

Bram shook his head. "It wasn't her," he said.

"She didn't come?"

"Someone came," Bram said. "It wasn't her."

He ducked his head, obviously unwilling to continue this thread of the conversation. But Clare's hope made her greedy. "How do you know?" she pressed.

Bram stared out at the bright line of the horizon. "My father told me to put on a jacket and trousers," he said. "But I wasn't wearing socks, and there was butter on the jacket. She never noticed. My mother would have."

"Maybe," Clare suggested, "she was thinking about something else. Something more important."

Bram shook his head.

Clare's own jaw set. The hope of speaking with her father was too strong to let him dismiss.

"But did it sound like her?" she asked. "The things she did say?"

"It didn't sound like anything," Bram said. "Just an old lady talking in a dark room."

"Well, the Sensitive speaks," Clare said, but even as she fell into Bridget's mother's familiar vocabulary, she realized that no Sensitive was required for Jack to speak to her. "But what did she *say* to you?"

"It wasn't my mother," Bram said again, his voice as sharp as she'd ever heard it.

Stung, Clare snapped back. "I heard you before. But how do you know?" Her voice rose as she spoke, and broke high on the last word at something dangerously close to tears.

Instantly, Bram's face softened. "Hey," he said, in the voice she knew. "I'm sorry."

In return, Clare swallowed some of her own hope. "Maybe it wasn't her," she admitted. "I just don't see how you can be so sure."

Bram's blue eyes traveled over her face like a pilot checking the wind and the horizon.

"Because she came back," he said.

"Came back?" she repeated. A storm broke in her heart: hope, that if Bram's mother had come to him, her father could come back too, and hurt, that Bram's mother had returned to him, but her father had never come for her.

But when she searched Bram's face for an answer, she only saw defiance and shame, as if he'd just confessed a dirty secret.

"Where did she find you?" Clare demanded. "When did she come?"

"She was just waiting outside the house," Bram said. "One day when I came out."

"You were by yourself?"

Bram nodded. "She told me she'd been waiting," he said. "Until I was alone."

"What did she tell you?" Clare asked.

"She said she didn't want to leave," he said. "She said one day I'd understand." At the thought of those words from her own father, comfort settled over Clare. But Bram's lip curled in anger, like a man's did when he'd been tricked.

"Are you sure it was her?" Clare asked. "How did you know?"

"She's my mother," Bram said, with faint surprise that this required explanation.

If Bram could see his mother, Clare wondered, why couldn't she see Jack? "She looked just like anyone on the street?" she said. In that case, she thought, ghosts might walk among them all the time, and nobody could ever tell the difference.

"She looked the same as she always did," Bram said. "But she was wearing a new dress." Anger rose in his voice at this.

Clare had felt the same anger since her father's death.

But even though she still wasn't sure who deserved it, she'd learned enough to know it wasn't him. "It's not their fault," she said gently. "No one can help when they die."

Bram glanced up, his eyes wary and confused. Then understanding dawned in them. "No," he told her. "She's not dead. She never died."

The death of Bram's mother was such an established fact in Clare's world that she couldn't take this in at once. To accept it meant all the other facts she knew had to strain and shift, and all other truths suddenly became precarious. It took a long, dizzy moment for her to even form a question.

"Does your father know?" she asked.

Bram nodded. "He didn't want to tell me she left," he said. "I guess he didn't know where she went. He might have thought she really died. Or maybe he wished she did. We were in Italy. It wouldn't be hard to get papers."

"Did you tell him?" Clare asked. "When she came back?"

Bram shook his head.

"Never?" Clare said. "But what if she comes back again?"

"She never did," Bram said.

Dread filled Clare's heart at the weight of the secret he had carried so long on his own.

"Does Denby know?" she asked.

"I never told him," Bram said.

He'd shifted on the carpet as they talked, so that instead of looking out to sea, he seemed to be trying to shoulder the ocean out of the conversation.

She had forgotten her hands on the sandy rug until he reached for one. When he took it, the skin on her shoulders and arms and shins woke up, as if they were all waiting for their own touch.

Overhead, somebody laughed, followed by a shriek of false alarm from Bridget.

Clare snatched her hand back. She scooted away from Bram on the rug, then scrambled to her feet. Bridget, Teddy, and Denby were halfway down the path, close enough that they might have seen everything, but far enough up that they could have missed it all.

As Clare watched, Denby lunged after Bridget, who led the procession, and caught her in an awkward hold. Bridget gave another lusty scream, broke free, and darted down the next turn in the path. Teddy loped along behind them, taking occasional swigs from a flask.

Clare let out a long breath. Bridget was a good actress, but not that good. If she'd caught sight of Bram as he held Clare's hand, she would never have been able to play her role with Denby so well.

"Clare," Bram said. He stood now too, barefoot on the rug.

Bridget skidded around the last rocky turn and slid onto the beach.

Clare had been right. The sight of Bram and Clare broke Bridget's concentration completely. Her smile vanished. Her chin came up and she crossed her arms.

But to Clare's surprise, the same expression also appeared on Denby's face when he caught sight of the two of them. He didn't give Bridget another glance. Instead, his eyes flicked between Bram and Clare, measuring and calculating with all the same jealousy as Bridget. But while Bridget's transformation from shock to rage had been complete, Denby pressed his lips together to hold back an unmistakable hurt that Clare had never seen cross his face before.

"That's not the one I told you to get," Denby said, nodding at the rug like a prince presented with a gift so small it insulted his high rank.

"I told you," Bram said. "Someone would miss the one from the sunroom. And then they'd miss everything."

Without a word, Bridget stalked down to the water and started out over the rocks, alone.

"I guess it's better than nothing," Denby said, and started after her.

Teddy slid down onto the beach as Denby left. "Bram!

Clare!" Teddy exclaimed. The cynical twist that usually marked his face was gone, replaced by the eerie eagerness of a slow child. His voice was urgent and loud.

It took Clare a minute to place what had happened to him. She knew the symptoms well enough among her mother's friends. She'd just never seen them in someone her own age. When Teddy grasped her in a clumsy hug, his fingers groping her waist, the whiskey on his breath confirmed it.

Clare shoved him away with all her strength. Teddy laughed as if she'd just told a spectacular joke. "I didn't interrupt, did I?" he asked. "You two seemed to be having such a *good time.*"

"We weren't—" Clare began, then struggled for words. "—doing anything," she finished.

The flash of pain in Bram's eyes only lasted an instant, but it was so clear that Clare felt an answering pain in her own chest. He knelt and began to roll the rug up over the sand.

Clare turned back to Teddy to see if the lie had at least convinced him, but Teddy had already lost interest. He tottered down the beach toward the rocks.

Bram hoisted the rug over his shoulder and stood. The roll of wool and jute drooped over his shoulder. Clare reached to help but couldn't get a good hold.

"I've got it," Bram told her.

She couldn't see his face beyond the bulk of the rug, so she circled to his other side as he went down the beach.

"Bram," she began.

"You don't have to explain anything to me," he said.

SIXTEEN

A HANDFUL OF PLAYING CARDS erupted from a deck on the carpet beside the sea-foam divan as Clare stepped into the glass house.

"Where have you been?" Jack demanded.

Clare threaded the maze of mismatched furniture to the divan, where she settled down, let her shoes fall from her feet, and pulled her legs up under her.

Jack's voice came from above her now, as if he had stood while she sat.

"What's this?" he asked.

"What?" Clare said.

On the floor, one of her shoes spun around like the hand of a watch being wound, and stopped with its toe pointing back at her, so that the bloodstain from the day she cut her foot, still a fresh dark red, stood out plainly on the pink satin lining. The edges of the stain were blurred by salt water. "*That*," Jack said.

This was not how Clare had imagined the conversation would go. She tried to dismiss the question with a curt answer. "I cut my foot," she said.

"When?" he asked.

"Before," Clare said. "On some rocks at the beach."

"Let me see," Jack said.

The command rankled Clare, but his concern softened her. She untucked her foot and turned the sole up. The cut was worse than she remembered, a narrow trench between the ball and heel, so deep that the scab inside only filled it partway.

She heard a sharp intake of breath. When Jack spoke, his voice was indignant.

"They didn't give you a bandage?" he asked.

"There was no one there but us," Clare said.

"Us?" he repeated.

"My friends," Clare told him. "None of us had bandages."

"They should have gone and got someone."

"We were going to a hidden cave," Clare said. "We didn't want anyone to find us." As that excuse hung in the air it seemed to weaken, even to her. "Bram helped me," she added, to ward off a growing sense of foolishness.

"Who's Bram?" Jack asked.

"One of my friends," she said. But she had hesitated.

Her shoe toppled from an invisible kick. It listed on its side against its twin. "Your boyfriend?" Jack asked.

Clare fought the same sensation of drifting into unknown waters she always felt when these questions arose. She shook her head, half in answer, half against the feeling.

"Does he want to be?" Jack demanded.

"I don't know," Clare said.

Apparently her confession of ignorance was not the answer he wanted. The deck of cards splayed out over the carpet in a tantrum of suits and faces. Then the room went silent.

In the silence, Clare recalled her own cause for indignation.

"I met Jack Cunningham the other day," she said.

Jack's voice, usually so cocksure, was suddenly cautious. "What do you mean?" he asked.

"An old man named Jack Cunningham," she went on. "He used to work here."

Overhead, a gust of wind blew the sheltering leaves aside. Light poured down through the vines. Clare raised her hand against it. When the wind died and the shade returned, Jack still hadn't spoken.

"Jack?" Clare said.

"I'm here," he answered, from the floor.

His tone was so subdued that Clare felt a twinge of remorse. But it didn't overcome her outrage at his lie.

"Do you know him?" she asked.

A card rose from the floor, one edge still buried in the carpet, as if, at a tense moment in the game, Jack wanted to double-check what he held in his hand. It was a face card, the royal heads turned at unnatural angles on their gaudy necks.

"What's your name?" Clare asked.

The card fell over on its back. Its faces gazed up unblinking through the glass.

"I don't know," he said.

This possibility had never even crossed Clare's mind. But the instant he admitted it, her memories dropped into place the way a deck of cards fell together in a dealer's hands: his sidesteps when she pressed for details, his retreats into pranks and plans, his reticence about the past. Still, she couldn't quite believe it.

She had woken up in dozens of strange rooms, not certain what country she had slept in, or what season it was beyond the new window. She'd forgotten things she desperately wanted to remember, like the sound of her father's voice as he promised her a good night. But no matter how far she'd traveled or how deep her fatigue, she'd never forgotten her own name.

"What do you mean?" she asked.

"I remember other things," Jack offered. "I used to live in the big house. I know all the rooms. When the light comes on above the workshop, I know it's Tilda."

Clare glanced up the hill. She had never thought to wonder where Tilda went each night. The red roof over Mack's workshop did form a peak high enough to hide a good-sized room, with a pair of windows that overlooked the garden. But all this could be just another story, like his name.

"But there's no door," she said.

"There is," Jack said. "By the stairs down from the kitchen. There's another set of stairs next to them, side by side. They go up to her room."

Clare had never spent any time in that dark corner of the shop. There might be a hidden staircase there, or there might not.

"What about your mother?" she pressed.

One of the playing cards twitched at her feet. "I know where I want to go," Jack insisted. "I know what a boat looks like when it leaves harbor."

"Do you know her name?" Clare asked.

"No," Jack admitted.

"Or your father's?" Clare asked.

The strain was clear now in his voice. "I think I used to know," he said. "I think it's getting worse."

"How could you forget?" Clare asked.

"I don't know," Jack said again.

The lace hem of her skirt shifted, as if a faint wind had stirred it.

"I don't forget you," he said.

Clare felt a touch, light but undeniable, on her fingers. She drew her hand back, startled.

"Could you feel that?" Jack asked, his voice high with surprise.

Clare nodded.

"Wait," Jack said. This time the touch was more deliberate: a fingertip drawn across her knuckles, then traced over the back of her hand in a spiral that wound tighter with each revolution. She shivered.

"I'm sorry," Jack said. His voice had gone soft in wonder. "I never tried to touch anyone before. I didn't know I could."

A faint weight covered her entire hand now, as if a leaf had fallen onto it from a tree above. It had none of the heat of Bram's hand, but warmth spread through her from it, as if a tide had turned in her blood, drawing it all toward that place with stronger and stronger waves.

Then the touch was gone.

Clare glanced around the glass house, but her eyes were no help.

"Don't be scared," Jack said. His voice came from above now, as if he'd stood up but stayed close.

She felt faint pressure against the side of her leg as he settled beside her on the divan. Then something like a shawl settled over her bare shoulders.

Clare's balance deserted her. She felt as if, with the slightest move, she might begin to drift and tilt like a feather in the breeze.

Another touch guided her head toward Jack's unseen shoulder. At first she held back, not certain it could support her. But it did, not with the steady warmth of her mother's breastbone, but like a pillow that first sank and then lifted her head. The faint weight of his hand covered her own again.

She took a shaky breath and closed her eyes.

SEVENTEEN

TILDA CUT A THICK daub from the cloud of raw meringue and transferred the sweet foam grimly to the pastry bag beside the metal trays that waited on the counter.

A few weeks earlier, Clare's mother had taken it into her head to cook something in Tilda's kitchen. Commandeering the kitchen of their current residence had become one of her favorite pastimes over the last few years. When they first began, Clare had hoped these occasional flurries of domestic activity might indicate a buried longing for home, but so far they had resulted in nothing but an eclectic series of culinary experiments, all accomplished with her mother's characteristic stubbornness and excess: sleepy errand boys sent out at midnight in search of saffron or white pepper, clouds of flour billowing from broken sacks, fine water glasses pressed into service as measuring cups or mixing bowls, and of course, all the kitchen's finest ingredients devoted to a dish that up to that minute had been on no one's menu but her own.

Maids on several continents had tolerated this behavior. Her mother had made cucumber sandwiches in Venice, cinnamon toast in the Antilles, and mint lemonade for two dozen guests of a visiting rajah she'd befriended in Greece. She had fried chicken in California, and spent an entire morning straining her own mozzarella to top half a dozen pizzas on the coast of Maine.

But when she'd swept into Tilda's kitchen one morning with the blithe announcement that she just felt like whipping up a little something, Tilda had stopped her cold.

"I'm afraid that's impossible," Tilda had said.

"Impossible?" Clare's mother had repeated. This was the same word that had triggered the exodus from Clare's childhood home, and when Clare, who had followed her mother into the kitchen, heard it, she retreated to the chair by the window, certain a storm would follow.

But Tilda's rough-hewn features bore a resolution the servant girl at Clare's childhood home had lacked. And Tilda hadn't lost track of the fact that, despite any claims she might make to her own domain, she was still a servant. "This is hardly the kind of kitchen where you'd like to cook," she said, to excuse her refusal. "I spent the last forty years working on that stove, and it still singed the lace off my best apron last winter. Just when you think you know all its tricks, it learns another one."

"Well, I wasn't thinking of anything too fancy," Clare's mother began, starting for the icebox. "I'm sure if I just look at what we have here, I can find—"

Tilda had planted herself between Clare's mother and the white enamel cabinet. "There's nothing in there but the beets and the butter beans for dinner," she said. "I order it fresh every day."

Clare knew the expression on her mother's face: a bemusement that could turn, with the faintest provocation, into either laughter or a tantrum.

Tilda tipped the balance by phrasing her next salvo as a request. "Why don't you just let me know what you'd like, and I'll take care of it?" she suggested.

"Well, I wouldn't expect you to know how to make anything quite like this," Clare's mother returned.

Tilda arched her eyebrows, which was almost as startling as watching the same expression cross the face of a stone figure who presided over the entrance to a hall of justice. "You might be surprised," she said.

Outmatched, Clare's mother still proved a tough negotiator on the terms of her surrender. "I was just remembering a crème brûlée I had this spring in Paris," she said. "It's just a simple custard, except that I believe it's finished with a torch. Do you think you could come up with something like that?"

Tilda nodded, unflinching.

"The restaurant flavored it with lavender," Clare's mother had mused. "But I was thinking it might be delicious with rosewater. So perhaps you could just make us some of both."

The next morning, an iron tank with a merry red hose had appeared in the corner of the kitchen, and that evening Tilda laid a pair of perfectly glazed crèmes brûlées at each of their places, one garnished with a sprig of lavender, one with the spiky oval leaf of a rose.

But Clare's mother had not accepted a quiet defeat. Since then, every few days, she'd appeared in the kitchen, craving a catalog of sweets that veered quickly from actual memory to pure fabrication. Clare had, in fact, shared a lavender crème brûlée with her mother the day before they left Paris, but she had no recollection of the dozen-layer cake of jelly and lady fingers, sliced paper thin, that her mother ordered next. And Clare knew she'd never seen the flock of swan-shaped meringues her mother had opined about this morning, allegedly glimpsed through the window of a tiny bakery on a side street in Bruges, or was it Amsterdam, with anise seeds for eyes and a dust of peach sugar to color their bellies.

Tilda touched the metal tip of the pastry bag to the wax paper that lined the first cookie sheet. A bud of meringue blossomed into the solid body of a swan, the curve of its breast swept back to the point of a delicate tail. Then she placed the tip of the pastry bag against the half-formed creature's breast and, in a single graceful motion, drew its long neck and drooping head. But it was only after she provided the new swan with a pair of neatly folded wings that she looked up at Clare and broke into a smile.

This was the first time Clare had seen Tilda smile. The effect was jarring, because it was beautiful. It was a child's smile, with none of the self-consciousness of a woman who offered her smile as a weapon or gift, and none of the calculation of a man who smiled to win his point or seal a deal. Tilda's smile was so innocent that Clare felt ashamed for her, and protective, the way she felt about younger children who hadn't yet learned the things she already knew.

"What do you think?" Tilda demanded as the smile faded back into her face's familiar lines. "Does it measure up to the Dutch?"

"Even better," Clare said, despite the fact that the Dutch pastries, as far as she knew, had never existed.

Tilda wet her finger, selected an anise seed from a small bowl beside the cookie sheet, and gave her creation sight. She spun the sheet on the counter to apply the opposite eye. Then she picked up the pastry bag again and provided her original swan with a perfect mate.

Clare had just come down from the boy's room, where she'd been on a hunt for any clue to Jack's real name. She'd prowled through the empty closet, pushed aside the tin soldiers in his desk, checked the speller and notebooks for a signature, but found nothing more than a half-finished translation of a Greek naval campaign.

Even as she'd searched, she'd half known it was useless. She liked to make up stories based on the evidence earlier guests sometimes left in hotel rooms: a sequin, a cigarette burn, a phone number scrawled through the price of drinks on a menu. But they were only ever enough to dream, not to understand someone, or find them. Only somebody who had known them could tell you that.

"How did you learn to do that?" Clare asked Tilda now.

After her first pair of swans, Tilda had become sure-handed as she filled the wax paper with a small flock of frothy birds. Still, she was so occupied that she might not be on guard. And this question, Clare hoped, was vague enough not to raise an alarm but still draw Tilda back into the past.

"The same way I learned everything else," Tilda said. She finished one bird's wing and began to form the belly of another.

"Your mother?" Clare guessed, hoping to snare her in sentimental recollection.

Tilda gave a shard of something like laughter. "My mother had three before me and seven after," she said. "She taught me to stay out of the way."

"So you taught yourself?" Clare tried: an attempt at flattery.

Tilda wouldn't be taken in by this, either. She gave her head a firm shake. "The young missus," she said. But her eyes softened.

Every other time Clare had tried to probe a flash of feeling from Tilda, Tilda had clammed up. So this time Clare stayed silent, like a hunter waiting for an animal to forget the sound of his footstep in the woods.

Her ploy worked. A moment later, Tilda went on without a prompt. "She got tired of bread pudding," she said. "I'd only been here a week. Bread pudding was all I knew to make."

"She taught you," Clare said, her voice low, so as not to break the spell.

When Tilda shook her head this time, the gesture was

almost girlish. The trace of youth playing over her worn frame was spooky. It had never occurred to Clare before that Tilda must have been young once, too. Clare's heart twisted at the thought, but she wasn't sure if it was because Tilda had once been young like her, or because one day she would be old like Tilda.

"She said I should surprise her," Tilda said. "And order anything I wanted from the farmers or from town. I thought I was a rich girl."

"What did you make?" Clare asked.

"A lemon cake as heavy as a brick," Tilda said. "Angel food cake without any sugar in it. Mack put butter on that and ate it for bread. He ate it all, everything we couldn't send to the big table."

Tilda's manner was so free as she said this that Clare decided to risk a direct question.

"What about the boy who lived here?" she asked. "What did he like?"

All traces of youth vanished from Tilda's face. She gave Clare a hard look.

"We don't speak of the dead," she said.

It was clear from her tone that she considered this the end of the conversation. But Clare quickly saw the advantage she'd just gained. Tilda hadn't just admitted that a boy had lived in the house. She'd also admitted that he was dead.

"Dead?" Clare said. "Did something happen to him?"

"That hardly matters," Tilda said. "You're dead just the same."

Clare swallowed, trying to calculate how she could have lost the upper hand so quickly, and what she could do to win it back.

"My father died three years ago," she blurted.

This fact, she knew, virtually guaranteed unconditional surrender. Her mother's friends murmured it to one another and bowls of strawberries appeared at her place or carousel gates swung open even though the ride had closed. But she had never used her father's death to her advantage until now. The price was too high. His loss drained the pleasure from the berries and carousels and tangled them in weird shadows. She had never wanted those shadows to infect anything else. So when the words escaped her lips she froze, startled.

Tilda didn't blink. "My father died before I could talk," she said. "I used to play with some buttons of his, but then my brothers took them."

Clare didn't know if she had been neatly outplayed or if Tilda had just told her a genuine confidence. She stared into

Tilda's eyes as if they were windows to a room whose door Clare couldn't find.

Tilda swept up the baking sheet, turned her back to Clare, and shut the birds inside the oven.

EIGHTEEN

JACK?" CLARE SAID.

She pulled the door of the glass house shut behind her, her skin tingling.

In the day since Jack first touched her hand, she had discovered that her memories of him worked very differently than her memories of her father. The things she remembered about her father grew weaker and more strange each time she called them up, like paper melting in the rain. But each time she remembered Jack's touch, all the same warmth she'd felt at first flooded back. In fact, it seemed to grow stronger each time she thought of it. And it didn't just grow stronger. It created false memories or dreams. Jack had never touched her face, but when she thought of his hand on hers the memory bent, and suddenly the featherweight of his finger brushed her cheek, followed the line of her lip, dropped to the weird bones that met below her chin. And these new dreams didn't wait for her to call them up. They broke into all her other thoughts. She couldn't escape them, but they also kept her company everywhere she went.

Now that she stood in the glass house again, though, she realized with an uncomfortable shock that Jack wasn't just a memory she carried with her. He was a whole boy, with ideas of his own, whose form she couldn't even see to reach for.

A hand touched her arm. Another one brushed her cheek.

"Tag," Jack said. "You're it."

Clare had never liked tag, even when the other players weren't invisible. So she employed the same strategy that she did when other children tried to tag her into their games. She walked over to the sea-foam divan, and sat down.

A moment later, Jack settled beside her.

As his fingers threaded through hers, she said, "You're it."

Immediately, Jack's fingers began to twist in hers. She tried to hold on but he slipped free, not the way she had pulled her hand from Bram's, but the way water sank into sand.

Before she could even miss him, though, his arm slid over her shoulders.

"Now *you're* it," Jack said.

"No," Clare said, her hand on his invisible knee. "I've got you."

He tapped her arm. "Got you back."

"But I still had you," Clare argued, and squeezed his knee to remind him.

Jack's other hand covered hers on his knee. "You're it," he insisted.

Now they were thoroughly tangled together. "We're both it," Clare said. "We both win."

"That's not how you win," Jack said.

Wrapped up with him, Clare felt Jack's weightlessness infect her again. This time it didn't come with vertigo, but hope. With his hand on hers, everything felt possible. Why shouldn't she also walk through walls?

"I went up to your room the other day," she murmured. "But I couldn't find anything that told your name."

His touch was so light it was hard to tell, but she thought she felt him shift away. She waited for him to settle back.

"What's wrong?" she asked, when he didn't.

In answer, he pulled completely free of her.

Stung, Clare sat up.

"Don't you care who you are? I thought you'd want to know," she said.

A twinge told her this was only half true. She'd wanted

to know. She hadn't thought whether he would or not, until now.

"Why do you care so much?" Jack burst out.

Clare stared into the empty space where he had been.

Jack's voice softened. "I can be any boy you like," he said. His invisible hand found hers again. "I can be a prince if you want a prince. And if you want to go to sea, the next day I can be a sailor."

Clare's mind toyed with this lamp of endless wishes. But she already knew him: his pranks, his itch to explore, his bragging and gifts. Even without a face, he was too vivid to erase and remake each day.

"But you *are* somebody," she said.

Jack's voice was quieter than she had ever heard it.

"What if you don't like him?" he asked.

Clare lifted a hand to his face. Her fingers brushed the skin under his invisible eyes, then spread until her thumb found his mouth. Jack let out a sigh like the last sound a child makes before he's finished crying.

With only her hands as a guide, Clare pressed her lips to his.

She felt him press back, not warm and firm like her mother's kisses, but the way water caressed her skin when she floated in the ocean, holding her up although she could never hold it. This lack only seemed to make the new heat under her skin flare hotter, asking for something she didn't have the words to name. It was stronger than anything she had felt before, except pain.

Confused, she turned her face away against his shirt. His light touch smoothed her hair.

"I never kissed anyone before," he told her.

"How do you know?" she said.

Jack laughed. But when he answered, his voice was serious. "I know it like I still know all the places I want to go," he said.

"I never did either," Clare told him. The heat inside her mellowed to warmth, but as it left it seemed to take some part of her with it. She glanced up the hill at the windows Jack said were Tilda's.

Jack kissed her temple. His arm circled her shoulders.

As it did, the unseen mist that ringed the glass house seemed to flicker up around them in Clare's mind, like a single stray frame cut into the reel of a movie. At the thought of it, her greed to see her father stirred.

"What's it like," she asked, "when you go in the mist?"

Jack drew a lazy eight on the bare skin of her shoulder, then brushed it away.

"You can't see anything," he said. "It's like you're walking at night, but the night has turned white."

"How far have you gone?"

"I don't know," Jack said. "It's hard to tell."

"I could get some string," Clare suggested. "Thin string, so it would be easy to carry. We could tie it to a tree and you could take it with you."

"I don't like to go into the mist," Jack said. He sounded like a child, confessing a fear.

But Clare's imagination, which had furnished the yard with unseen mist, now began to furnish the mist with wonders. And hope made her pitiless. "Don't you want to explore it?" she asked.

"It's nothing but mist," Jack insisted.

"You can't be sure of that," Clare said. "You've never gone far enough."

"What do you know about it?" Jack retorted. "What do you think I'd find?"

"Well," Clare said. "You're not the only person who ever died."

Jack's arm vanished from her shoulders so quickly that she wondered for an instant if her words had cast an inadvertent spell that threw him back into the other world.

"Jack?" she asked.

He must have gotten up in agitation, because now he spoke from above her. But his voice was low, as if for fear of being overheard. "There's someone in there," he half whispered.

Clare's heart lurched with hope.

"Who?" she demanded.

"I don't know."

"What do they say?" Clare asked.

"Nothing," Jack said. Each of his answers was more re-luctant.

"Do they touch you?" she asked, with a thrill of horror.

"No," Jack said. Frustration crept into his tone.

"Then how do you know they're there?"

Jack dropped his voice even lower. "The way you know someone's in a room," he said. "Even when they don't say anything."

Involuntarily, Clare dropped her voice as well. "Do you think they might hurt you?" she asked.

"No," Jack said immediately.

Clare spread her hands in exasperation. "Then what are you afraid of?" she asked.

"It's hard to come back," Jack told her. "When you go too far in."

"You get lost?" Clare asked.

"No," Jack said. "The mist sort of—pulls you in. The farther you go, the stronger it gets."

"Then where do you meet this person?" Clare asked, cir-cling back to the clues that might lead to her own father.

"He's always there," Jack said. Then his voice leapt. "Who's that?"

Clare had the sickening sense that another spirit had just joined them in the room. She gave a violent shudder.

But when her head jerked around, she saw her mother walking across the lawn, straight toward the glass house.

Clare crouched in the shadow of one of the wing chairs.

"My mother," she whispered.

There was no time to say more. While her mother's view was still obscured by the trunks of the maples, Clare scrambled out of the glass house. She circled the back, screened by the thick vines, and came around the front just as her mother reached the glade.

"Clare!" her mother crowed. "Tilda thought you might be around here somewhere."

Clare hid a grudging smile of admiration. Tilda had never caught Clare in the glass house yet, but she hadn't given up.

"Come on," Clare's mother said. She caught Clare's hand and led her back around to the hidden door.

When they reached the mossy flagstone, Clare's mother stared through the etched glass. "It's beautiful, isn't it?" she said.

Warily, Clare nodded.

Her mother took the leaf-handled key from her pocket and slotted it in the lock.

Clare lurched forward, swiping for the key. "What are you doing?" she cried.

Her mother looked down, startled. "We're just going to take a look inside."

"But they don't use this house anymore," Clare insisted. "Tilda said. Remember?"

Her mother dismissed Clare's protest with a wave. "Oh," she said. "I talked with her about that when she gave me the key. Why in the world *wouldn't* they use a summer house this beautiful? She couldn't give me any good reason."

Her mother turned the key. The door swung open.

Clare's mother took in everything there was to see with a sharp eye: the wing of the piano, the couch and chairs scattered on the overlapped rugs, the books at large between them. But the instant she stepped inside the glass house, a wave of vertigo washed over Clare. For the first time in her life, she knew something her mother didn't, not just a child's secret or a small detail, but a fact that changed everything. Clare had always had to sort her mother's various pronouncements, discard dramatics, filter for moods. But until now it had been her mother's voice that named the world and made a thing true. Clare had always been able to take refuge in the certainty that, when it mattered most, her mother would know what to do. But her mother couldn't know the answers here, because she couldn't see the truth.

"Well," her mother said appraisingly. "I think this should do."

A square of stationery dropped from the buffet to the floor. Clare scanned the limbs of the candelabra, the varnished wood, the rich carpet below. It was impossible to tell if the page had been blown by wind from the open door, or if it was one of Jack's tricks.

Her mother toed one of the books on the floor. "If they straighten this all up and light some candles, it might even pass for a Venetian palace," she said. "We'll just have to make sure no one arrives until dusk."

"Arrives?" Clare repeated.

Her mother slid her arm around Clare's waist. "We're going to have a party," she said. "Everyone's been needling me all summer about why we didn't take a place on the coast. So I told them last night to come over and we'd show them."

Clare took an anxious glance around the room for a reaction from Jack.

"I thought you'd be happy," her mother said, a hint of uncertainty in her voice. "You seemed so fascinated by this place when we first came."

"It's fine," Clare hurried to say.

To her relief, her reply didn't fool her mother. She smoothed Clare's hair back ruefully. "You used to be so much easier to please," she said, and kissed her.

NINETEEN

EVERY MORNING, TILDA WAGED a brief but futile war to put Clare's mother's room back into something approaching order. And every day, within five minutes of Tilda's departure, Clare's mother undid all Tilda's best efforts with a dexterity and inventiveness that hinted at the presence of an artist at work. Today, before she left the house for a luncheon, Clare's mother had thrown a peach silk robe over one of the rods that supported the room's crisp white curtains. Splayed out, the voluminous folds of fabric added a new layer of scrim to the window dressing, but also a sense of alarm: the fabric was so close to the color of her mother's skin that it gave the impression a human figure stood in the window. A dragon, embroidered in red thread, prowled the back of the robe, infuriated to find himself upside down and helpless.

Clare crossed by him gingerly, to the big wardrobes where her mother's things were hung. Below a knot of stockings, in the skirts of her mother's gowns, under an assortment of enamel cigarette cases and jewelry boxes, her fingers closed around the spine of a suede and paper photograph album.

She pulled it free gingerly, like an archaeologist extracting ancient treasure from the rubble. Then she carried it back to her own room, where she settled down cross-legged on the small rug by her window.

Clare hadn't held the album since her father's death. But she did have memories of it. When she was small, her mother had used it to tell her stories, like with any other picture book. But unlike other picture books, these stories changed with each telling. Sometimes the changes were small: a feather on a hat her mother remembered once as turquoise, once as red. Others posed more jarring contradictions: a pale-eyed young man, caught by the camera in the midst of a laugh, who had been killed by gas the first week he went to war, or perhaps just caught the flu. A lake that sometimes lay south of Chicago, and sometimes in northern Michigan. A girl who waved from a black horse in an apple orchard, and shifted from a friend to a stranger and back again, depending on who told the story: Clare's mother or her father. Her mother was the better storyteller. But her father's stories, Clare had recognized even then, had the strong advantage of being accurate.

In those days, she hadn't been able to fathom how her parents could prefer these small dark images to all the flash and color of actual life. Even her mother's wedding portrait, with its silver lace and perfect studio halo, couldn't compete with the flush that came up in her mother's face each time she began a new story.

Back then, the album had seemed lifeless.

Now it felt haunted.

Clare folded the soft suede cover back to reveal the first page: a snapshot of her father at the end of a dock, his face blurred by a smile.

To her surprise, her face broke into an answering smile. She turned the page.

Her father grinned up from an Adirondack chair. Behind him, spikes of hollyhock jutted up like a rakish crown. He strutted along the ledge of a high stone balcony. He approached down a long lane, swinging a bunch of flowers wrapped in newspaper the way a ballplayer might bring his bat up to the plate.

Her mother appeared for the first time in the bow of a canoe. The sun overhead had been so bright that it ate up the horizon so her mother seemed to drift from the surface of the lake directly into the sky. After that, the pictures of her father and mother mingled. In one, her mother stood with her back against a tree. In the next, her father had climbed into its branches, his pale jacket in a heap on the grass below.

Clare had braced herself for sorrow, but she was powerless against the happiness that washed through her with each glimpse of him. She'd wanted to look at him with eyes wiser than a child's, but the sight of him turned her childlike again.

When she reached the end, she let the cover fall back into place. But it didn't blot the images out. Instead, they crowded together in her mind and came alive. And instead of satisfying her desire to speak with her father, they made it grow wild.

Clare closed her eyes.

She'd heard Bridget's mother insist again and again that to reach into the spirit world wasn't magic, but science. It was only simple conversation, with an advanced method of listening.

So with her eyes still closed, Clare let a single word glow and echo in her mind: *Daddy?* As her mind spoke, her lips parted, but no sound passed between them.

Someone came into the room.

Clare knew without a doubt that the person who had joined her was not her father, just as she knew without a doubt that she was not alone. Immediately, her eyes sprang open.

Nothing in the room had changed. Even the clouds seemed to be frozen to the sky. But the sense that she was not alone didn't fade. Instead, it grew stronger.

"Hello?" she said aloud.

A surge of love swept over her, so strong it was difficult to catch her breath. With it came the sense she got from Tilda's sharp looks, that she'd been recognized for who she was, and not the pose she'd chosen. But this feeling went even deeper: that whoever had joined her knew everything she'd ever done, things her own father couldn't know, things even she had forgotten.

But she didn't know a thing about it.

The terror of this brought her to her feet. She left the album askew on the floor, darted into the hall, and pulled the door shut.

But the presence was just as strong on this side of the door as it had been in her room. It didn't fade when she rattled down the stairs, or when she burst from the front hall onto the porch, or fled the porch for the lawn.

It wasn't until she stopped in the shade of the front oaks, her breath ragged, that the presence receded. But she didn't have any sense that she'd outrun it. Instead, it seemed to have left her. And when it did, she felt a new kind of loneliness, for something she couldn't name, like the feeling from a dream erased by waking, with her sore heart the only proof. She gazed around the yard, half hoping the presence would return.

When it didn't, she headed over the lawn, toward the glass house. But when she rounded the corner, its door stood open, propped with a garden hoe. Half its contents had been spread under the maples, where Mack wandered through the empty chairs and couches with a strange blend of tenderness and suspicion, as if he were the only living guest at a party for ghosts.

TWENTY

THE SPIRITIST LAUGHED.

"Well, you know," he told Clare's mother, as the nearby guests looked on from their mismatched armchairs and divans. "It's very unusual to find a presence out of doors."

Clare glanced at the glass house. One object of the party had been to show off its weird charm, but by the time the guests had arrived at dusk, the glass hulk with the candlelight leaking out between the vines had taken on the aspect of a giant coal burning up from the inside. The few guests who had ventured through the shadows to the half-hidden door had found a dim, empty room whose walls seemed to be made from slabs of night. Almost no one who dared to make a circuit of the house ventured inside, and the few who did hurried out again to rejoin the party, which had collected on the furniture Mack had scattered under the maple canopy, between comforting strings of electric lights.

Bridget's mother sat beside her spiritist on a leather settee. Bridget's father sat opposite them on the sea-foam divan. Clare's mother sat at the foot of the divan, separated from him by a respectable length of cushion. Clare stood just outside the circle, in the shadow of the glass house.

"Oh," Clare's mother said, with extravagant disappointment. "But I was sure you would find us a ghost tonight. None of us have seen anyone but each other since May. We're all so bored we could spit. You're sure there's absolutely *no one* out here?"

Bridget's father and mother hadn't exchanged a word all night, but they both turned to Clare's mother at this. Bridget's mother scanned her face with the sharp eye of a true believer grown suspicious of praise through long years of ridicule. Bridget's father glanced at her with the sudden unease of a doctor who has just discovered a warning symptom in a patient he'd believed to be healthy.

Clare's mother kept her gaze fixed on the spiritist, a young man whose remarkably fine suit was strangely at odds with his eyes, which were bold but wary, like a street child's. The instinct to maintain his dignity struggled on his features with a showman's desire to please. Around the gathering, the conversation dwindled as guests turned to observe.

"I'm sure," Clare's mother prompted him with disarming confidence, "if there *was* anything here, you could feel it."

"Well, of course," the spiritist agreed.

Clare's mother leaned forward with an eagerness that almost disguised the malice in her eyes.

"Would you try?" she asked.

Bridget's mother tried to give the spiritist a warning glance, but by now he was in Clare's mother's grasp.

He continued to protest, but only for show. "I'm not sure everyone would be interested in—"

"Nonsense," Clare's mother interrupted. "What could be more interesting than eternity?"

The entire party had gathered around them now, with two exceptions. Bridget stared stonily at the sky, her legs draped over the side of one of the red wing chairs in a stand of furniture the other guests had abandoned as they gravitated toward the spiritist. Nearby, Teddy took advantage of the distraction to add the contents of his pocket flask to a glass of Tilda's mint lemonade.

Amanda Bradburn, a doe-eyed girl with a wide mouth and a nervous laugh who had joined them at the seaside that summer after an ignominious stint at a finishing school in Philadelphia, swept into the open seat between Clare's mother and Bridget's father. She gave Clare's mother a look of open derision as she arranged the filmy layers of her dress, then settled back against the divan.

Clare scanned the faces of the other guests to see if any of them had taken in this broad commentary on the friendship between her mother and Bridget's father. She caught Bram's figure on the far side of the circle, his back to the hill. His eyes met hers. Beside Bram, Denby caught the motion. He searched the gathering, his gaze alert, but didn't settle on any face.

"Shall we get you anything?" Clare's mother asked. "A candle? Or a bell?"

The spiritist set one hand on each knee and gave his head a curt shake.

"He is the instrument himself," Bridget's mother explained, in a tone of scientific rebuke.

"Forgive me," Clare's mother said. But by now the drama was unfolding without her help. The spiritist closed his eyes. Clare's mother leaned back to watch.

Unseen fingers threaded through Clare's. She started. From across the crowd, she could feel Bram's eyes on her.

"Watch this," Jack said, low in her ear.

She shook her head and reached for him, but only caught the corner of his invisible jacket as he brushed past.

Fear coursed through her. She didn't know what powers

the spiritist might command. If he discovered Jack, could he hurt or banish him?

The spiritist took a long breath. Around the circle, the crowd drew in their own.

For a long moment, nothing stirred. Then the tip of the spiritist's tie twitched faintly, as if in a private breeze. But the spiritist, locked in his drama of communion with the other world, didn't flinch, or even seem to notice.

Clare's mother's eyebrows shot up in amusement at the trick, mingled with grudging respect.

Then the young man shuddered, as if an unseen hand had settled on his shoulder.

The crowd gave a blunted moan of fright.

Clare's hands closed helplessly at her sides.

The spiritist's head jerked as if someone had yanked it by the ear. His eyes sprang open. The crowd lurched back. For an instant, the spiritist's face blazed with raw challenge, like any cornered man's.

But as he took in all the eyes still fixed on him, he mastered his fear with admirable showmanship. His hands settled back on each knee. He squared his shoulders and let his chest swell under his well-cut vest. "There is a spirit here," he announced, in a tone that made it clear that any surprise he had felt was only the bemusement of an expert confronted with an unusual specimen.

Clare's mother leaned forward.

"What kind of spirit?" she asked. Clare could tell her mother still thought she was only playing a part in a magic show. But Clare could barely draw a breath as she waited for the spiritist's answer.

He took a moment to gauge the crowd. "A woman," he said.

Almost instantly a hank of hair stood up on the top of his head, as if someone had given it a healthy tug. The spiritist's face contorted with pain. Both his hands flew up to the spot, first to ward Jack off, then to smooth the hair down. Bridget's mother stared at him with horror and fascination, like a priest confronted by a living god whose actual speech contradicted all his beloved cant.

"What does she want?" Bridget's mother asked.

The young spiritist had not worked his way into the best circles of society by insisting on mystery when his client demanded answers. But he also knew better than to trap himself with specifics. He relied, wisely, on what he had already gleaned of the spirit's behavior. "To touch us in this world," he said.

"She must be lonely," Clare's mother said. "Do you think she would take my hand?"

The young spiritist measured Clare's mother, still uncertain if she was a convert or a heckler. "It requires sensitivity, and training," he began.

"Won't you just let me try?" Clare's mother asked, and held her hand out over the grass. "What should I do?"

The young spiritist checked the crowd again and gave in. "Close your eyes," he said.

Clare's mother obeyed, her hand still extended.

An unseen arm circled Clare's waist. She felt the brush of Jack's cheek against hers. "Come on," he said, with a gentle tug back into the darkness that surrounded the glass house.

Across the crowd, Bram gave Clare a questioning frown.

"I don't feel anything," Clare's mother announced.

"It may be very faint," the spiritist prompted.

"Come on," Jack said again, then vanished into the dark.

Around the crowd, eyebrows rose and lips curled. Figures began to shift, restless. The spiritist's reaction to Jack's teasing had been so genuine that it made the rest of his act ring false.

"I felt something just then," Clare's mother said. "But it might have been the wind. How do you tell the difference?"

Bridget's mother's eyes narrowed.

A few guests drifted toward the buffet where Tilda had arranged her cakes, tiled with candied rose petals and violets. The hum of voices began to rise into the dark leaves.

The spiritist glanced around the thinning crowd, no longer gauging their response, but as if wondering where the next blow might come from.

Clare waited until Bram, still on the other side of the party, turned away from her to hear something Denby said.

Then she walked backwards into the darkness, following the curve of the glass house until she came to the door, where she slipped in.

TWENTY-ONE

THE CONTENTS OF THE glass house had been shuffled so thoroughly that when Clare first stepped in she wasn't sure it was the same place. Of all the familiar furnishings, only the piano, buffet, and a few chairs remained, pushed back against the glass walls. The books had been stacked in neat piles on the buffet, the silver vases filled with daisies. Only the carpets, free of furniture, still lay in familiar layers. Even the light was wrong. Instead of filtering down through the leaves, it streamed from a dozen tapers in the chandelier overhead. Its light made the carpets glow like gems, but the whole house seemed to tremble each time the flames guttered in the wind.

Jack laughed in welcome as she stepped in. But without furniture to blunt the sound, his voice bounced from glass to glass so that it was impossible for her to tell where it had come from.

Clare frowned.

The head of one of the daisies from the buffet popped off and began to weave unsteadily toward her through the air.

"Do you think he'd like a flower?" Jack asked, his voice still full of glee from his prank on the spiritist. "The door's open. I could carry it out."

Clare disarmed him in a single motion.

"I'd rather you had it, anyway," Jack said. "You're prettier than him."

Clare cupped the daisy in her hand so the petals wouldn't break, and ignored the compliment.

Undeterred, Jack tried a distraction. "Watch this," he said.

A moment later, the chandelier lurched, then began to dance. The flames jerked and flattened in the sudden wind. Crystal drops clanged against the chandelier's glass branches. Hot wax rained down on the carpet below.

Clare sprang back.

"Clare," Bram said from the door. "Are you all right?"

The chandelier gave one final clumsy swoop, then began to rock back to stillness, like a swing after a child abandons it.

Bram came across the carpet and laid a hand on the small of Clare's back. Heat from it bled through the thin fabric of her dress. "What happened?" he said.

"Aren't you going to introduce me to your friend?" Jack asked.

Bram started. His gaze swung around the room. When it found nowhere else to settle, it returned to Clare.

Before she could answer, Bridget and Denby pushed into the glass house. Bridget clutched Denby's hand, but both of them stared at Bram.

Instinctively, Clare stepped away from him. When she did, she knocked into Jack. She could feel her shoulder crash into his chest, and the brush of his jacket on her hand. His fingers twined through hers.

She looked down to see if her hand gave anything away. It didn't.

Denby looked up at the black dome around them. "You hardly need to come down to the cave, Clare," he said. "You've got your own right here."

Clare bristled. "It's not like a cave," she said. "During the day."

"I thought your mother said they hadn't opened it all summer," Bridget said with a sharp look.

Behind her, Teddy appeared in the door. In his rumpled white suit, lit up by candlelight, he glowed like an apparition. "I bring spirits," he announced, pulling a silver flask from the striped lining of his jacket with a grand and sloppy flourish. "Spirits and libations."

He offered the flask to Denby. Denby took it, slugged back a gulp, then lifted his chin against the burn as he handed it back.

Teddy held the flask out to Bram. Bram glanced at Clare, a question still in his eyes. But he walked over to take it.

Bridget reached for the flask as Bram finished. He lifted it high, out of her grasp, and looked at Teddy.

Teddy smirked and shook his head. "Sorry, little sister," he said. "I'm not so drunk I'm going to serve you your first whiskey."

"It's not my first!" Bridget insisted, and made another grab.

Bram passed the flask to Teddy over her head. Teddy secured it in his jacket pocket again. "Who gave you whiskey?" he asked. "The librarian at the ladies' club?"

Beside Clare, Jack stifled a laugh. Clare glanced at Bram, but if he had heard anything, he didn't show it.

Bridget retreated to Denby with the air of a mistreated soul appealing to her only protector. She collected his hand, then checked to make sure she still had Bram's attention. "We could play a game," she suggested. "What about post office?"

"It's just one room," Teddy pointed out. "There's no place to go."

"There's the whole forest," Bridget countered.

Teddy shook his head dismissively. "It's a kid's game," he said. "And Clare's never even kissed anyone."

All the eyes in the room fastened on Clare.

Clare's own eyes only widened for a moment, but that was enough.

"Wait," Bridget demanded. "*Have* you?"

Jack lifted Clare's hand, kissed it, and let it fall. To the rest of them it must have looked like a gesture of helplessness.

Teddy began to laugh.

Bridget stared at Clare, her eyes wide and undefended. Hurt was such a foreign expression on Bridget's face that Clare could barely recognize it. She stared back, struggling to understand what had wounded her friend.

Then Bridget turned the same injured look on Bram, and Clare knew.

Bridget's math would have been perfect if she hadn't forgotten to calculate on the hidden world. It had only been a few weeks since Clare had been forced to admit she'd never kissed anyone. Who else could Clare have kissed since then, besides Bram?

Almost as quickly as the hurt had appeared in Bridget's eyes, it winked out, replaced by cold fury.

"Bridget," Clare said, and stepped toward her.

"What?" Bridget demanded.

"It isn't what you think," Clare said.

"What do I think?" Bridget snapped.

"It's a ghost," Clare began. "The boy—"

Now Bridget's eyes narrowed with disbelief and rage. "Those lies won't work on me," she said. "I've heard them all my life."

She glanced around the room and discovered Denby only a step away. She seized his hand so they stood shoulder to shoulder like a pair of Jack's tin soldiers lined up for battle.

"Come on, Denby," she said. "We'll play our own game."

She pulled him out of the glass house, into the night.

Teddy let out a burst of ferocious laughter. He caught Clare around the waist and pressed in for a sloppy kiss. She turned her head so his lips met her cheek, not her mouth, but the smell of liquor still filled her throat. "I knew it, princess," he said, his face so close that her eyes couldn't focus. "I always knew all about you."

Clare slammed the palms of both her hands against his chest.

Still laughing, he released her. He brushed at the side of his face as if to shoo away some creature that had landed there. Then he executed a graceful bow and turned for the door. As he shambled across the room, he swatted a few more times at some invisible annoyance. Then he disappeared into the night.

Clare turned to Bram, who had stood by this whole time but not raised a hand to help her. She had thought she might find anger or derision in his eyes. Instead, he seemed lost.

"So, you," he said haltingly. "And . . . Teddy?"

"No," Clare said. "No, no."

The surge that had given her the strength to fend off Teddy had left her shaky. Her limbs felt strangely light. She had a strong impulse to catch Bram's arm, lay her head on his chest, and close her eyes. But he was looking at her like a worried child.

"But then," he asked, ". . . who?"

His hand flew to his ear and his face twisted in sudden pain. A moment later, he flinched again. This time he swatted at his other ear. Then he stumbled forward, as if someone had pushed him from behind.

"Jack!" Clare said, slapping at the air beside Bram. "Stop it!" She found the faint mass of Jack's torso, but when she tried to catch at it, he slipped through her hands.

Bram ducked as if something had just struck him in the face. His eyes sought Clare's, begging an explanation.

"Jack," she said again, glaring into thin air.

This time Bram jerked as if someone had landed a blow to his ribs. His expression turned dark. He scanned the whole glass house again, still empty except for Clare and himself. Then he headed for the door.

Clare followed. When Bram slipped into the night, she felt Jack catch her hand.

"Where are you going?" he asked.

Clare brushed past without an answer.

Outside, the knot around the young spiritist had disbanded. Guests stood now in small groups beneath the maples. Bram cut through the party and up the hill. He didn't stop until he had reached the garden below the kitchen windows, where he turned and saw Clare.

She climbed the last steps to the crest, breathless.

"Clare," he said. His eyes gleamed like water in the dark. "What was that?"

"I'm sorry," Clare said.

"Who's Jack?" Bram asked.

"He's just—" Clare began, then hesitated. "Just a boy," she said. "Who lives in the glass house." She took one of Bram's hands and pressed both hers to it, palms flat on either side. Compared to Jack's touch, Bram's hand was so solid and warm that it made everything around them seem less real. The big house beside them receded. The voices of the guests faded under the trees.

As gentle as ever, Bram pulled free. "Clare," he said. "That's not just a boy down there."

Then he went back to the party, hands in his pockets, leaving her alone in the dark on the hill.

TWENTY-TWO

CLARE SLIPPED OUT OF her room to return to the glass house a few hours after the last guest left. By that time, the country darkness was so deep that it was hard to see her own feet. The ground was invisible except for the occasional sheen of dew. With each step she took, the house on the hill behind her seemed to lurch like a ship on rough water.

Worst of all, the memory of the presence that had followed her down the stairs clung to her so strongly that she wasn't sure if it was a memory or if the presence itself had returned. The sense that it might have joined her again came with the same terror as before, but now there was a strange comfort to it as well. Whoever it was, she was not alone in the dark.

In the glade, the shadows were so thick that she couldn't see the lock on the glass house. She opened it by sense of touch. Inside, at least, the furniture had been put back where it belonged.

Before her eyes could pick the books from the buffet, find the chandelier on the ceiling, and untangle everything from the shadows of the vines, Jack pressed her to him in a full embrace. He caught her hair in his unseen hands and cupped her face to kiss it. She bowed her head against his next kiss with the sense that if she didn't, it might carry her across some unseen boundary into a new country she could never leave.

"I'm sorry," he said.

Clare hadn't known, when she'd pushed her covers aside, whether she was going to the glass house to demand an apology or to give one. She'd spent the remainder of the party deep in regions of the garden she knew were filled with mist for Jack, half furious at him for his outburst, half guilty that she'd abandoned him. But in the quiet of her room, both the accusations and the excuses faded into a simple ache to see him.

"I have something for you," Jack told her. His arms released her. Then his voice came from the divan. "Over here."

She followed him over, and sank down on the divan. When she searched the glass house for him by day, it seemed mockingly empty. But darkness had the opposite effect. Now it felt like he might be part of every shadow.

With the faintest scrape, the shallow drawer of the low

table shuttled open. A thread rose from it, like a snake answering a flute. It took her a moment to recognize the chain of a necklace. As she did, the chain lifted free of the drawer, drawing a pearl in the shape of a tear. It swung before her like a hypnotist's pendulum.

Then it dropped into her upturned palms.

"It's beautiful," Clare whispered. "Where did you get it?"

"Outside," Jack said. "Someone left it in the grass."

"Tonight?" Clare asked. "We should give it back."

"No," Jack said. "I've had it longer than that."

The pearl twitched at the end of its chain.

"Put it on," he said.

Clare fastened the chain around her neck. When she ducked her chin, she could see the faint glimmer of the pearl against the tiny pleats that trimmed her bodice.

"I tried to come up the hill after you," Jack said. "I went farther than I've ever been."

"What happened?" Clare asked.

"The mist got darker," Jack said. "But then it started to fade, like I'd come to the end of it."

Clare's heart quickened. "What did you see?"

"I was afraid," Jack said. "So I came back."

Clare didn't realize she had been holding her breath until it burst out of her in a rush of frustration. "But what if it's wonderful?" she asked.

Up at the big house, a light came on. Clare froze, waiting for it to go off again. Instead another one lit up. Suddenly, all the windows were ablaze, not just in the upper story, but the ground floor as well.

Clare leapt to her feet. "They know I'm gone."

"They won't find you here," Jack said.

"I have to go," she told him.

Jack caught her hand as she slipped out the door, and trailed her until they reached the boundary of the mist between the lilacs.

"Good night," he said.

Clare ran on a few steps, then turned and ran back. Jack's arms circled her. She buried her face in his neck. "I'll be back," she promised, her voice high with childish tears.

"I know," Jack said.

Then she struck through the side yard, planning her story as the dew collected on her slippers. She hadn't been able to sleep. She'd thought a walk might help. She didn't want to bother anyone else, so she let herself out.

But as she came around the front of the house, she glanced through one of the windows, into the parlor. Bridget's mother sat beside the unlit fireplace on a gaily striped chair, her face pale. Even stranger, Bridget's father stood beside her, his hand on her chair. His eyes were full of dread, like a boy surprised in the middle of a daydream by a teacher's question.

Clare's mother stood with her back to the window, in her blue robe.

Clare climbed the stairs to the porch. The front door swung open without a sound. She crossed the empty hall to the parlor door.

As she did, Tilda swept in from the dining room. She wore a white wrapper and her long silver hair fell in waves down her neck. For some reason, she carried a pair of unlit lanterns.

Her brows drew together at the sight of Clare, but before Tilda could say anything, Clare pushed open the parlor door and ducked in.

All three adults turned, but their faces seemed to fall when they recognized her. Her mother gathered her up in an embrace so tight it hurt to breathe.

"Sweetheart," she said. "We were just trying to decide whether to wake you."

Tilda stepped in, lanterns aloft. "I found two of them," she said.

No one knew she had left the house, Clare realized. Nobody had even noticed that her slippers were soaked through.

Clare's mother drew her over by the fireplace, to Bridget's mother. Despite the late hour, Bridget's mother looked more awake than Clare had ever seen her. When Clare met her eyes, they welled with tears.

Clare looked at her own mother for explanation.

"Clare," her mother said. "Bridget is gone."

Clare felt the prick of fear, but it was tempered by caution. If Bridget had snuck out on her own, Clare didn't want to be the one to give her away.

"Did you ask Teddy?" she said.

Bridget's father cleared his throat. "Teddy isn't feeling well," he said.

Clare had seen Teddy climb the hill at the end of the night: under his own power, but unmistakably impaired. She wasn't surprised they hadn't been able to wake him when they found Bridget gone.

"They thought she might have come here to see you," Clare's mother told her.

Clare shook her head. "No."

"Please," Bridget's mother said. Her gaze was so direct that Clare felt as if she weren't just looking into her eyes, but into whatever was left behind after a person died. "Do you have any idea where she could be?"

TWENTY-THREE

OR THE FIRST MOMENT Clare stood on the dark beach, she had the weird sense that she'd finally found a desert. The glint of dim waves became the hints of distant hills, and the low roar of the surf blotted out all other sounds into a false silence. The cave, the bluff, and the homes above were lost under moonlit dunes.

Then her lantern caught the gleam of a channel in the damp sand and she was back on shore.

Clare's mother, Bridget's father, and Bridget's mother had all followed her down the switchback path, across the beach, to the rocks. But when Clare kicked off her shoes at the water's edge, they stopped. The tide was in. The rocks at the cave's mouth were slick with the dark water that surged around it.

"I can't see anything," Bridget's mother said.

"You stay here," Bridget's father ordered. "I'll go."

Clare's mother put her arm around Bridget's mother's

waist. A quick, knowing look passed between Clare's mother and Bridget's father.

Clare stalked off barefoot toward the rocks.

Bridget's father caught up to her, his feet bare, the cuffs of his linen trousers rolled up. "I can go first," he offered.

"You don't know where it is," Clare told him, and climbed out on the first rock.

Behind her, Bridget's father's lamp amplified her shadow into a giant on the cliff. Her own lantern gave out faint cries as it swung in her hand. She leapt from the first rock to the next with the courage of pride. But as soon as she had gone too far to turn back, she stiffened with fear. The next rock was barely visible in the dark. The surface she could see was wet and slick. And even if she reached it, there was nothing there to catch hold of, just the rock after it glinting beyond another span of angry water.

Her mind reeled back to the presence that had followed her out of the house, in the dark. Now, despite the fear it stirred in her, she missed it.

"Are you here?" she whispered, lower than the wash of the waves.

The cliff, the rocks, the silver horizon: nothing changed. But suddenly the other ghost was with her again, this time far too strong to be mistaken for a memory. She felt the same rush of love and her own familiar fear. But this fear left no room for any others. Every one of them fell away before it. The noise of the waves no longer drowned her thoughts. The next rock was only a step away. And so was the one after it.

She only slipped once, just outside the cave entrance, on the last rock. Her foot plunged under the water and she fell hard on her hip. But she made the mouth of the cave before she felt any pain.

When she got her footing on the ledge, she reached back to help Bridget's father up.

Inside the cave, he raised his lantern above their heads. It illuminated the rough arch of the ceiling, a few feet of the ledge, and the narrow glint of water that cut back into the dark.

The two of them stood side by side like a pair of tourists struck silent by the scope of a new cathedral.

"Bridget?" Bridget's father said. It wasn't a call or a command. His voice had a tone of wonder to it, as if he couldn't quite believe that the place was real, or that his daughter had any part in it. Her name shimmered for a moment before the plash of water on rock swallowed it up.

The other ghost, Clare could feel, had followed them into the cave. Or, she thought, it was already there.

Bridget's father began to advance along the ledge.

"Bridget," he said again, his voice loud with the sound of a man trying to frighten something that frightened him.

The high, raw keen of an injured animal filled the cave so completely that it seemed as if it might be the voice of the darkness itself.

When it broke off, Bridget's father stood frozen. His eyes darted from rock to rock.

Clare brushed past him, ran down the ledge, and ducked through the cleft into the hidden room.

Her lantern was too weak to illuminate the whole dome of the giant chamber. The light only revealed a small ring in every direction: a hint of the wall behind her but not the one beyond, the fingers of rock that reached down, but not the ceiling itself. Something, she realized, like the mist that ringed Jack into the glass house.

"Hello?" she called.

She thought she heard a shuffle in the darkness, but then it went still.

As she pressed on into the cavern, the furniture emerged from what had been solid shadow. A cushion had fallen from the couch onto the rock. One of the chairs was turned akimbo, facing out into the dark.

"Bridget," Clare said.

Another rustle. Clare raised the lamp and followed it. After a few steps, her light picked out the looming curve of the far wall. A few more steps, and one of the large formations on the ground came alive.

Clare threw the lamp up in self-defense.

Bridget's face rose from the rock. In the low light, with the pale wall behind her, her head seemed to move free from a body under its own strange power.

Then her dress took shape. It was the same one she had worn to the party, layers of eggshell voile and cotton lace. The ribbon at her waist was loose. The lace was damp and stained. Her dark curls hung around her face.

Clare knelt on the smooth rock and set her lantern between them. She held out her hand. Bridget stared at it and then back at Clare's face, as if she were trying to make out a sign in a new language.

Far behind them, Clare heard a footfall at the chamber entrance. Another pinpoint of light glowed on the other side of the room. "Bridget?" her father said, his voice awed and uncertain.

Bridget's eyes fastened on the approaching light.

"Over here," Clare called.

The other lamp swung toward them through the dark. When Bridget's father caught sight of her, he fell to his knees on the stone.

Bridget held out her arms. Her father gathered her up and staggered to his feet. Bridget clung to him with the wordless tenacity of a child too young to speak.

Bridget's father carried her across the chamber, leaving Clare behind. But as his lantern dimmed with distance, she could feel again that she was not alone. The other ghost was here as well. There didn't seem to be any place she could go that it couldn't follow her.

Unnerved, Clare reached into her pocket for the wax key. Comfort washed through her as her fingers closed on the handle.

But as she traced down the stem, the stem ran out. It took her a moment to understand that it had snapped in half. And one more fumble to find that the thick teeth that fit the lock to the glass house had broken off.

Twenty-Four

Bridget's father stopped beside her bed, Bridget still in his arms.

Outside Bridget's open window, the surf seemed to catch its breath, then sigh.

Bridget's mother turned on the lamp by Bridget's bed. She bent to pull off Bridget's ruined shoes.

When she'd dropped them to the floor, she started to unfasten the line of covered buttons at the back of Bridget's dress.

Bridget shook her head. Then she began to struggle in her father's arms. "Put me down," she said.

"You're not—" Bridget's mother began.

But Bridget's father threw back the covers of the bed and laid her in it, still fully dressed. Sand sifted onto the sheets. He pulled the quilt up and tucked it under Bridget's chin.

In the doorway beside Clare, Clare's mother followed all his gestures.

Bridget turned her face to the wall.

"Would you like some warm milk?" Bridget's mother asked. Her eyes were still alert, but now they couldn't seem to fasten on anything. "I'll bring some milk," she said, and left the room.

Clare sat down on Bridget's bed.

"Cynthia," Bridget's father said. "Could I speak with you?"

Clare's mother followed him into the hall. He pulled the door closed behind them.

Clare found Bridget's hand under the blanket and covered it with her own.

Bridget stared at the wall as if it were a screen she could see things on. "He didn't know what to do," she said.

"Denby?" Clare asked.

"He pulled my hair and pinched my arms," said Bridget. "I told him to stop, and he threw me down. Then he took the light with him when he went."

She turned to look at Clare. Her pupils had grown so big it seemed like some of the darkness of the cave must have crept into them.

"It was so dark," she said. "I found the wall. I was going to follow it, but then I thought, What if I choose the wrong way, and I get lost inside the cliff? What if there's a pit, and I fall into it?"

The door opened. Teddy stood in it wearing only a pair of striped pajama bottoms. Bare, his chest was thin as a boy's.

"Bridge?" he said. His voice was still thick with drink, but it had lost its mocking edge. "What's wrong?"

Clare braced herself as he stepped into the room, but he didn't come near her. Instead, he took up a post at the foot of the bed.

"Is she all right?" he asked Clare.

Clare's mother appeared in the door behind him. "Clare," she said. "It's time to go."

"I'll drive you back," Bridget's father said from the hall.

"It's not far," Clare's mother said. "We can walk."

"It's the middle of the night," Bridget's father said. "Don't be ridiculous."

Clare rose. Then, as her mother had done so many times before, she leaned down and kissed Bridget's forehead.

Bridget closed her eyes.

As Clare went out, Bridget's mother carried in a mug of milk. A faint plume of steam trailed from it as she passed. When Clare glanced back, Bridget's mother stood over her daughter's bed, looking down with the wide eyes and stiff face of a woman who has seen a ghost.

TWENTY-FIVE

RIDGET'S FATHER PULLED AROUND the kitchen drive and cut the engine off.

Clare fumbled for her door handle, found it, and hopped out. She had her mother's door open before Bridget's father could get there from the other side. He circled the back of the car just as her mother stepped out.

He had left the headlights on. They called the white curve of the drive up out of the dark, but where the light gave out, Clare couldn't find a single glint or shadow to prove the yard hadn't been swallowed up by the same black space that hung between the stars.

She stood stubbornly beside her mother. But to Clare's surprise, he didn't look at her mother, but at Clare.

"How old are you?" he asked.

"Twelve," Clare answered.

Bridget's father nodded, as if this were a sum he needed to work a complicated calculation. Then he looked at her mother. "Did she ever do anything like this?" he asked. He didn't wait for an answer. "I just don't understand," he went on, "why she would do a thing like that."

"Robert," Clare's mother said. "Why did you do all the things you've done?"

He gazed at her with a look of dawning horror.

"This is very late for Clare," her mother said. "I should take her in."

"Of course, of course," Bridget's father repeated.

Clare's mother turned her cheek for him to kiss. He tried to nod at Clare but his eyes couldn't find a place to rest, as if she were an apparition that kept changing shape around the edges. "Good night," he said to something just over her head.

Inside, Tilda stood at the counter, fully dressed, her gray hair tucked up in its tidy bun. A pie shell stood beside her, filled with paper-thin slices of apple arranged in a precise spiral that wound round on itself like a staircase at the Vatican. From another sheet of dough, she was cutting delicate petals to create a flaky blossom that would cover the whole face of the pie.

"Oh, Tilda," Clare's mother said. "You didn't need to wait up for us."

Tilda's fierce expression made it clear that she hadn't stayed up to wait on them.

"We found Bridget," Clare told her. "We took her back home."

Tilda managed to drop her gaze before relief unmanned her.

Clare's mother gave Tilda a searching glance. "Did you know Bridget?" she asked.

"She tried to take a fifth of whiskey home in her skirt tonight," Tilda said. "But I caught her before she left."

She tossed a puff of flour at the round of dough that would become the top crust. "It's a terrible thing to lose a child," she added, and lifted the dough over the sugared fruit.

"But your apples," Clare's mother protested. "No one will see them."

When Tilda glanced up this time, her expression was simply startled, as if she couldn't understand why a fact so obvious bore mentioning. Then she dropped the crust over the intricate spiral, fluted the edge with her fingertips, and distributed the dough petals into a sunburst that nodded at the end of a delicate stem.

She folded her arms across her wiry frame. "I guess you've seen better than this," she said. "In London or Paris."

"No," Clare's mother said. "I haven't."

Clare and her mother climbed the stairs to their rooms in silence. At the landing, her mother kissed the top of Clare's head. Then she slipped into her own room and Clare went on to hers.

Without turning on a lamp, Clare kicked away her damp, gritty shoes, peeled off her stockings, and traded her ruined dress for a clean nightgown. She slipped the chain of the pearl under her collar.

When she turned to crawl into her bed, her mother's shadow filled the open door.

Clare shuddered.

Her mother gave a low laugh. "Ah, honey," she said. "I didn't mean to scare you."

She folded back the covers and Clare got into bed. Her mother sat down beside her, pulled the covers back up, and laid her hand on Clare's face.

"You've grown so much," she said.

A stubborn knot formed in Clare's chest, just under Jack's pearl: the same knot that always formed when anyone made the threat that she could not remain a child. But her mother's words called something up out of the knot, like one of the vines that grew over the glass house, blind but determined to climb.

Clare gave a single nod.

"I was thinking," her mother said, "that we should go home. How would you feel about that?"

Clare had held her own all night against the dark and fear, but at the mention of home, her eyes filled with tears.

"But what about," she began, to test the hope against the biggest obstacle she could imagine. "What about Robert?"

In the shadows, her mother's brow furrowed. Then she began to laugh. She leaned over and kissed Clare's cheek, still laughing. "Oh, honey," she said. "Oh no. No, no. He's been fraternizing with Amanda Bradburn all season. Didn't you see her at the party? How she came to sit between us?"

"But you're always—" Clare said.

Her mother bowed to nuzzle Clare's cheek. "Dear God," she said. "No. He talks with me because I'm the least likely woman on this whole coast to fall in bed with him, and his wife knows it. She never gives him trouble about me, and nobody bothers me when I'm with him. Honey," she said, and the amusement in her voice faded to remorse. "I can't believe you've been worried about this."

Clare linked her fingers with her mother's in the dark.

"So do you think you'd like it?" her mother asked. "If we went home?"

Clare felt the pull of the glass house in the yard below,

but it had already started to grow faint, the way even the loudest sounds faded down to the whisper of the tracks as you pulled away from them on a train.

"Yes," she said.

TWENTY-SIX

SO MUCH SUN POURED through Clare's windows the next morning that at first she thought the whole wall of her room must have turned to glass. She pushed the covers away and went over to the blinds, which she'd forgotten to pull the night before. Faint mist rose from the garden into the cool air below. The panes of the glass house were hazy with it. According to the clock beside her bed, it was even earlier than she usually woke.

She traded her cotton gown for the first simple dress she found in her closet.

In Jack's room, she crossed quickly to his desk. The little glass of tin soldiers was in the drawer where she had found it last.

But the key was gone.

Clare poured the tin men out on the desk. She sifted through the entire company, just to be sure. Then she settled them back in the glass, one by one.

She already knew what had happened to the key. Tilda must have used it to open the glass house for the party.

The kitchen, when Clare reached it, was deserted. All the platters for the party, the dozens of glasses, the pits and stems of fruit, the soiled napkins, had vanished. The only evidence of the previous night was Tilda's pie, which stood on the high counter in the center of the room, now baked flaky gold.

Clare checked for the key in the drawer of towels. When she didn't find it there, she went on to the next drawer. She pushed aside ladles, basters, and table utensils. She peered into the depths of saucepans and griddles on their dark shelves. She stuck a butter knife into the bowl of salt by the stove in case the key was buried at the bottom.

Then she left the knife in the sink and padded down to Mack's workshop. Just as Jack had said, she found a second door at the foot of the stairs. Like everything else in the shop, it was covered with a film of dust. But beneath that, the wood was finer than the other rough furnishings of the shop, with the same insets and inlay as the doors inside the house. It had a solid brass knob with a simple lock. A thin band of light streamed through the keyhole.

Clare bent to put her eye to it.

As she did, she heard the low rumble of thunder. A shadow fell beyond the door.

Clare scrambled back in time to avoid a black eye, but not soon enough to escape or hide.

At the sight of Clare, Tilda stopped on the last step, in the open door. "What do you think you're doing?" she demanded.

Clare stared up, speechless. An entire summer of observation had left her with no more clue how to manage Tilda than she had when she first arrived.

Tilda's eyes narrowed. "Where did you get that?" she asked, and nodded at Clare's throat.

Clare's hand rose. She remembered that she still wore the pearl necklace Jack had given her at the same moment her fingers closed on it.

Distractions and excuses spun through her mind: curtseys, jokes, trivia, compliments. But the only thing she could find words for was the truth. And the truth didn't spin untethered in her mind. It weighed so heavy on it that any thought to disarm Tilda was lost in Clare's yearning to lay her burden down.

Tilda crossed her arms.

Clare struggled against it, but the temptation to confess was irresistible. "Jack gave it to me," she said.

"Jack?" Tilda repeated.

"He found it in the yard," Clare said, carried along by the relief of sharing a secret. "By the glass house."

Tilda's eyes remained narrow until Clare mentioned the glass house. Then they lit with understanding. She let out a breath she seemed as if she might have held for years. "His name isn't Jack," she said.

A jolt like the first step from warm sand to cold water went through Clare.

"What is it?" she asked.

"I told you not to go down there," said Tilda. "The day you got here."

"He doesn't know who he is," Clare said. "He can't remember his own name."

This fact seemed to bow Tilda's head. She turned back on the narrow stairs. "Come with me," she said.

Clare scrambled up after her.

The room was sparsely furnished with a simple bed, dresser, and stuffed chair. The bed and chest of drawers were both painted white, and a white sheet had been thrown over the chair. The gold grain of the wood floor, a small braided rug, and a bed quilt pieced from jewel-box tints provided the only color.

Tilda knelt on the rug to pull a round hatbox from under the bed. She settled on the mattress, the box balanced on her knees, and began to rummage through a sea of loose cards and photographs.

From these, she fished a case a little smaller than a deck of cards, with an embossed leather cover. A tap of her finger undid the catch to reveal wine-colored velvet on one side and the flash of a mirror on the next. The mirror was clouded with something.

Tilda handed it to Clare.

When Clare held it in her hands, the image of a boy appeared on the mirror, his features captured in silver. He was older than her, perhaps Teddy's age, with pale hair and gray eyes. Clare tried to find an answer in them: the trace of a smile, or the shadow of a thought, but his eyes just searched hers, asking his own questions.

"What happened to him?" Clare asked.

"The fever came on a ship," Tilda said. Something in her tone gave Clare the idea that the truth came as a relief to her as well. "The port doctor put them on quarantine, but they were afraid to turn back the owner's son when he wanted to board. He went all over it. Up in the rigging. Down in the hold. He was fine the next day. But that night, it came on.

"She sat with him for three days running. But the third night she fell asleep. When she woke up he was gone. We never thought he could have gotten all the way to the glass house. He could barely stand without help. Mack only found him when the sun came up. By then it was too late."

When Clare turned the silvered glass, the image inverted. The boy's eyes disappeared and his hair turned black. She touched the pearl at her neck. "This was hers," she said.

Tilda nodded.

"Where did they go?" Clare asked.

"He took her away that same year," Tilda told her. "She died of flu during the war. He had a stroke a year ago. But his nephew kept us on to run the place."

Clare lifted the little case. "How did you know he was still there?"

"I heard the music through the glass," Tilda said. She glanced out over the garden. "I didn't like the idea of him out there all alone. And he was company for me."

Her eyes met Clare's. "I never understood why he stayed."

"He's afraid to go to heaven," Clare told her.

Tilda nodded as if this was a familiar disease.

"But it's heaven," Clare insisted.

Tilda raised her eyebrows, giving Clare the point. "But to go there," she said, "we have to leave everything we know. You spend your whole life learning to live in this world, and then this world is gone."

She began to collect the loose papers and photographs from the quilt. As she did, Clare picked up a grainy snapshot.

"It's Mack," she said.

He was so young in the picture that it had taken her a minute to place him, but he wore one of the same work shirts she'd seen him in all summer long. He held a flowering plant up for the camera, its roots cradled in his palms, which were black with soil.

Tilda retrieved the photograph and deposited it in the hatbox. "Not anymore," she said, and dropped a sheaf of papers on it.

"You love him," Clare said, reckless from all the other secrets they'd shared.

"Of course I do," Tilda retorted. "No one was ever kind to me like Mack. From the day I came here, he never let me carry a stick of firewood in. Before that, I can't remember a day I didn't. He'd bring me feathers and pretty rocks he found in the yard. When his mother died, no one else could make her whiskey cake. So I kept trying until he said mine was good as hers.

"He asked me to make it when he married Addie," she added. "That was the first I heard about that."

"I'm sorry," Clare said.

Tilda let the lid settle over the scraps in the box. "None of us ever get all the things we want," she said. Her eyes met Clare's, full of a light of triumph Clare had only caught there in glimpses before. "But we can keep anything we want in our own heart."

Clare held out the silver plate, but Tilda shook her head. "That's yours," she said.

Clare let the velvet cover fall over the glass and fastened the album's sickle hook. "What was his name?" she asked.

"Nathaniel," Tilda answered.

Clare held out her hand. "I need the key," she said.

Tilda pulled it from her pocket.

TWENTY-SEVEN

A FILM OF GOLD DROPPED over Clare's face when she stepped into the glass house. Jack's lips pressed hers through the thin fabric.

Then the sheer veil rose and described a long, celebratory arc before it dropped into a gold puddle suspended in Jack's invisible hand.

"I got it last night," Jack crowed. He poured the scarf in a waterfall of silk from one unseen hand to the other. "I thought you'd like it, so I caught it when she sat down at the piano, and when she got up—" He trailed off. "What's wrong?" he asked.

"I'm going home," Clare said. Despite the tears that stood in her eyes, a smile twisted her lips.

"That's good," Jack said, his tone alert but bewildered. "It's where you wanted to go."

Clare nodded.

"Then why are you crying?" he asked.

"I can't stay," she told him. "You can't come."

Jack's lips met one of her tears and smeared it in a broad stripe across her cheek.

"I brought you something," Clare said. She pulled the leather case from her pocket. But when she tried to hand it to Jack, it lurched in his grasp.

"It's heavy," he said.

"Here," said Clare. She took her seat on the divan, laid the case down, and undid the clasp.

The tooled cover seemed to rise under its own power, slowly but steadily, until it stood perpendicular to the plate. Then it fell open. The boy's image stared up at them, half mirror, half shadow.

"What is it?" Jack asked.

"You," she said.

The case twitched and skidded on the old upholstery. "He's so thin," Jack said.

Each time the case jerked, the image inverted. The boy's face slipped into shadow, flared up, disappeared again.

"He looks like he might be brave," Jack added.

Clare reached, found his sleeve, and followed it to his hand.

"Where did you get it?" he asked.

"Tilda," Clare said. "She remembers you."

Jack's finger traced an infinite loop on the back of her hand.

"Are my parents—" he began.

"They're gone," Clare told him. "I'm sorry."

The worked leather cover of the case rose from the divan again. It fell over the image and blotted it out.

"Did she tell you my name?" he asked.

"Nathaniel."

Jack's hand went still on her own.

"Don't you like it?" she asked.

"It's a good name," Jack said, but the disappointment in his voice was unmistakable.

"Is it the picture?" Clare asked, and bumped the leather case with her knuckle. "I like it."

Jack's finger followed the arch of her brow to her temple, found the valley below her eye, and dropped down the slope of her cheek to her lips. Then he raised her chin and kissed her.

"What's the matter?" she whispered.

Jack turned the case on the green upholstery. "I thought it would tell us something."

"It did," Clare said. "We know your name. We can see your face."

"But what does that tell us," Jack asked, "that we didn't know before?"

Clare had wondered this same thing the day she met him. And she didn't have any better answer now than she did then.

Jack rose from the couch. "Maybe it doesn't matter," he said, and began to pace. "Maybe that's why I forgot."

"But you know now," Clare said.

"What if I forget again?"

A chill ran over Clare. "Do you think you'll forget everything?"

"I don't know," Jack said.

Clare looked up the hill at the garden that was lost in mist to Jack.

"Listen," she said. "The ghost in the mist."

Jack sat back down beside her and took her hand.

"I think it might haunt the whole world," she said.

"What do you mean?"

"It's in the house, too," she told him. "And the garden. And at the shore."

Jack's hand went still in hers. "How do you know?"

"I can feel it too," she told him.

"What did it do to you?" he demanded.

The other ghost had come for her when she called, and stayed with her in the dark. "It helped me," she said.

"Were you afraid?"

"Yes."

Something brushed her lips, landed between the bones at the base of her neck, took flight again.

"If I go up the hill," Jack said, "will you go with me?"

Clare nodded. "When?"

Jack was already on his feet, pulling her along with him.

His hand stayed firm in hers as they crossed through the glade and for the first steps beyond. Then, as they gained the hill, his touch began to fade.

"Jack?" she asked.

"I'm right here," he said.

A step later, he was gone.

Clare stopped in the early sun halfway up the hill. For a few breaths, she waited for him to turn back and find her again. Then a strange certainty settled over her: not just that Jack was gone, but that she was not alone.

She ran the rest of the way up the hill, toward the garden and sky reflected in the kitchen glass, which changed all the familiar shapes and made them shine so bright that they seemed like windows into another world.